Darkness & Dawn 1:
The Vacant World

**Other books by George Allen England
available from Leonaur**

Darkness & Dawn 2
Beyond the Great Oblivion

Darkness & Dawn 3:
The After Glow

Darkness & Dawn 1:

The Vacant World

George Allen England

LEONAUR

Darkness & Dawn 1: The Vacant World
by George Allen England

Published by Leonaur Ltd

ISBN (10 digit): 1-84677-034-3 (hardcover)
ISBN (13 digit): 978-1-84677-034-0 (hardcover)

ISBN (10 digit): 1-84677-027-0 (softcover)
ISBN (13 digit): 978-1-84677-027-2 (softcover)

http://www.leonaur.com

Publisher's Notes

The views expressed by the author do not necessarily reflect those of
the publishers.

In the interests of authenticity, the spellings, grammar and place names
used in this book have been retained from the original edition.

To Robert H. Davis
Unique inspirer of plots
Do I dedicate this, my trilogy
G.A.E.

1: The Awakening

Dimly, like the daybreak glimmer of a sky long wrapped in fogs, a sign of consciousness began to dawn in the face of the tranced girl.

Once more the breath of life began to stir in that full bosom, to which again a vital warmth had on this day of days crept slowly back.

And as she lay there, prone upon the dusty floor, her beautiful face buried and shielded in the hollow of her arm, a sigh welled from her lips.

Life -- life was flowing back again! The miracle of miracles was growing to reality.

Faintly now she breathed; vaguely her heart began to throb once more. She stirred. She moaned, still for the moment powerless to cast off wholly the enshrouding incubus of that tremendous, dreamless sleep.

Then her hands closed. The finely tapered fingers tangled themselves in the masses of thick, luxuriant hair which lay outspread all over and about her. The eyelids trembled.

And, a moment later, Beatrice Kendrick was sitting up, dazed and utterly uncomprehending, peering about her at the strangest vision which since the world began had ever been the lot of any human creature to behold -- the vision of a place transformed beyond all power of the intellect to understand.

For of the room which she remembered, which had been her last sight when (so long, so very long, ago) her eyes had closed with that sudden and unconquerable drowsiness, of that room, I say, remained only walls, ceiling, floor of rust-red steel and crumbling cement.

Quite gone was all the plaster, as by magic. Here or there a heap of whitish dust betrayed where some of its detritus still lay.

Gone was every picture, chart, and map -- which -- but an hour since, it seemed to her -- had decked this office of Allan Stern, consulting engineer, this aerie up in the forty-eighth story of the Metropolitan Tower.

Furniture, there now was none. Over the still-intact glass of the windows cobwebs were draped so thickly as almost to exclude the light of day -- a strange, fly-infested curtain where once neat green shade-rollers had hung.

Even as the bewildered girl sat there, lips parted, eyes wide with amazement, a spider seized his buzzing prey and scampered back into a hole in the wall.

A huge, leathery bat, suspended upside down in the far corner, cheeped with dry, crepitant sounds of irritation.

Beatrice rubbed her eyes.

"What?" she said, quite slowly. "Dreaming? How singular! I only wish I could remember this when I wake up. Of all the dreams I've ever had, this one's certainly the strangest. So real, so vivid! Why, I could swear I was awake -- and yet -- "

All at once a sudden doubt flashed into her mind. An uneasy expression dawned across her face. Her eyes grew wild with a great fear; the fear of utter and absolute incomprehension.

Something about this room, this weird awakening, bore upon her consciousness the dread tidings this was not a dream.

Something drove home to her the fact that it was real, objective, positive! And with a gasp of fright she struggled up amid the litter and the rubbish of that uncanny room.

"Oh!" she cried in terror, as a huge scorpion, malevolent, and with its tail raised to strike, scuttled away and vanished through a gaping void where once the corridor-door had swung. "Oh, oh! Where am I? What -- what has -- happened?"

Horrified beyond all words, pale and staring, both hands clutched to her breast, whereon her very clothing now had torn and crumbled, she faced about.

To her it seemed as though some monstrous, evil thing were lurking in the dim corner at her back. She tried to scream, but could utter no sound, save a choked gasp.

Then she started toward the doorway. Even as she took the first few steps her gown -- a mere tattered mockery of garment -- fell away from her.

And, confronted by a new problem, she stopped short. About her she peered in vain for something to protect her disarray. There was nothing.

"Why -- where's -- where's my chair? My desk?" she exclaimed thickly, starting toward the place by the window where they should have been, and were not. Her shapely feet fell soundlessly in that strange and impalpable dust which thickly coated everything.

"My typewriter? Is -- can that be my typewriter? Great Heavens! What's the matter here, with everything? Am I mad?"

There before her lay a somewhat larger pile of dust mixed with soft and punky splinters of rotten wood. Amid all this decay she saw some bits of rust, a corroded type-bar or two -- even a few rubber key-caps, still recognizable, though with the letters quite obliterated.

All about her, veiling her completely in a mantle of wondrous gloss and beauty, her lustrous hair fell, as she stooped to see this strange, incomprehensible phenomenon. She tried to pick up one of the rubber caps. At her merest touch it crumbled to an impalpable white powder.

Back with a shuddering cry the girl sprang, terrified.

"Merciful Heavens!" she supplicated. "What -- what does all this mean?"

For a moment she stood there, her every power of thought, of motion, numbed. Breathing not, she only stared in a wild kind of cringing amazement, as perhaps you might do if you should see a dead man move.

Then to the door she ran. Out into the hall she peered, this way and that, down the dismantled corridor, up the wreckage of the stairs all cumbered, like the office itself, with dust and webs and vermin.

Aloud she hailed: "Oh! Help, help, help!" No answer. Even the echoes flung back only dull, vacuous sounds that deepened her sense of awful and incredible isolation.

What? No noise of human life anywhere to be heard? None! No familiar hum of the metropolis now rose from what, when she had fallen asleep, had been swarming streets and miles on miles of habitations.

Instead, a blank, unbroken leaden silence, that seemed part of the musty, choking atmosphere -- a silence that weighed down on Beatrice like funeral-palls.

Dumfounded by all this, and by the universal crumbling of every perishable thing, the girl ran, shuddering, back into the office. There in the dust her foot struck something hard.

She stooped; she caught it up and stared at it.

"My glass ink-well! What? Only such things remain?"

No dream, then, but reality! She knew at length that some catastrophe, incredibly vast, some disaster cosmic in the tragedy of its sweep, had desolated the world.

"Oh, my mother!" cried she. "My mother -- dead? Dead, now, how long?"

She did not weep, but just stood cowering, a chill of anguished horror racking her. All at once her teeth began to chatter, her body to shake as with an ague.

Thus for a moment dazed and stunned she remained there, knowing not which way to turn nor what to do. Then her terror-stricken gaze fell on the doorway leading from her outer office to the inner one, the one where Stern had had his laboratory and his consultation-room.

This door now hung, a few worm-eaten planks and splintered bits of wood, barely supported by the rusty hinges.

Toward it she staggered. About her she drew the sheltering masses of her hair, like a Godiva of another age; and to her eyes, womanlike, the hot tears mounted. As she went, she cried in a voice of horror.

"Mr. Stern! Oh -- Mr. Stern! Are -- are you dead, too? You can't be -- it's too frightful!"

She reached the door. The mere touch of her outstretched hand disintegrated it. Down in a crumbling mass it fell. Thick dust bellied up in a cloud, through which a single sun-ray that entered the cobwebbed pane shot a radiant arrow.

Peering, hesitant, fearful of even greater terrors in that other room, Beatrice peered through this dust-haze. A sick foreboding of evil possessed her at thought of what she might find there -- yet more afraid was she of what she knew lay behind her.

An instant she stood within the ruined doorway, her left hand resting on the moldy jam. Then, with a cry, she started forward -- a cry in which terror had given place to joy, despair to hope.

Forgotten now the fact that, save for the shrouding of her messy hair, she stood naked. Forgotten the wreck, the desolation everywhere.

"Oh -- thank Heaven!" gasped she.

There, in that inner office, half-rising from the wrack of many things that had been and were now no more, her startled eyes beheld the figure of a man -- of Allan Stern!

He lived!

At her he peered with eyes that saw not, yet; toward her he groped a vague, unsteady hand.

He lived!

Not quite alone in this world-ruin, not all alone was she!

2. Realization

The joy in Beatrice's eyes gave way to poignant wonder as she gazed on him. Could this be he?

Yes, well she knew it was. She recognized him even through the grotesquery of his clinging rags, even behind the mask of a long, red, dusty beard and formidable mustache, even despite the wild and staring incoherence of his whole expression.

Yet how incredible the metamorphosis! To her flashed a memory of this man, her other-time employer -- keen and smooth-shaven, alert, well-dressed, self-centered, dominant, the master of a hundred complex problems, the directing mind of engineering works innumerable.

Faltering and uncertain now he stood there. Then, at the sound of the girl's voice, he staggered toward her with outflung hands. He stopped, and for a moment stared at her.

For he had had no time as yet to correlate his thoughts, to pull himself together.

And while one's heart might throb ten times, Beatrice saw terror in his blinking, bloodshot eyes.

But almost at once the engineer mastered himself. Even as Beatrice watched him, breathlessly, from the door, she saw his fear die out, she saw his courage well up fresh and strong.

It was almost as though something tangible were limning the man's soul upon his face. She thrilled at sight of him.

And though for a long moment no word was spoken, while the man and woman stood looking at each other like two children in some dread and unfamiliar attic, an understanding leaped between them.

Then, womanlike, instinctively as she breathed, the girl ran to him. Forgetful of every convention and of her disarray, she seized his hand. And in a voice that trembled till it broke she cried:

"What is it? What does all this mean? Tell me!"

To him she clung.

"Tell me the truth -- and save me! Is it real?"

Stern looked at her wonderingly. He smiled a strange, wan, mirthless smile.

All about him he looked. Then his lips moved, but for the moment no sound came.

He made another effort, this time successful.

"There, there," said he huskily, as though the dust and dryness of the innumerable years had got into his very voice. "There, now, don't be afraid!

"Something seems to have taken place here while -- we've been asleep. What? What is it? I don't know yet. I'll find out. There's nothing to be alarmed about, at any rate."

"But -- look!" She pointed at the hideous desolation.

"Yes, I see. But no matter. You're alive. I'm alive. That's two of us, anyhow. Maybe there are a lot more. We'll soon see. Whatever it may be, we'll win."

He turned and, trailing rags and streamers of rotten cloth that once had been a business suit, he waded through the confusion of wreckage on the floor to the window.

If you have seen a weather-beaten scarecrow flapping in the wind, you have some notion of his outward guise. No tramp you ever laid eyes on could have offered so preposterous an appearance.

Down over his shoulders fell the matted, dusty hair. His tangled beard reached far below his waist. Even his eyebrows, naturally rather light, had grown to a heavy thatch above his eyes.

Save that he was not gray or bent, and that he still seemed to have kept the resilient force of vigorous manhood, you might have thought him some incredibly ancient Rip Van Winkle come to life upon that singular stage, there in the tower.

But little time gave he to introspection or the matter of his own appearance. With one quick gesture he swept away the shrouding tangle of webs, spiders, and dead flies that obscured the window. Out he peered.

"Good Heavens!" cried he, and started back a pace.

She ran to him.

"What is it?" she breathlessly exclaimed.

"Why, I don't know -- yet. But this is something big! Something universal! It's -- it's -- no, no, you'd better not look out -- not just yet."

"I must know everything. Let me see!"

Now she was at his side, and, like him, staring out into the clear sunshine, out over the vast expanses of the city.

A moment's utter silence fell. Quite clearly hummed the protest of an imprisoned fly in a web at the top of the window. The breathing of the man and woman sounded quick and loud.

"All wrecked!" cried Beatrice. "But -- then -- "

"Wrecked? It looks that way," the engineer made answer, with a strong effort holding his emotions in control. "Why not be frank about this? You'd better make up your mind at once to accept the very worst. I see no signs of anything else."

"The worst? You mean -- "

"I mean just what we see out there. You can interpret it as well as I."

Again the silence while they looked, with emotions that could find no voicing in words. Instinctively the engineer passed an arm about the frightened girl and drew her close to him.

"And the last thing I remember," whispered she, "was just -- just after you'd finished dictating those Taunton Bridge specifications. I suddenly felt -- oh, so sleepy! Only for a minute I thought I'd close my eyes and rest, and then -- then -- "

"This?"

She nodded.

"Same here," said he. "What the deuce can have struck us? Us and everybody -- and everything? Talk about your problems! Lucky I'm sane and sound, and -- and -- "

He did not finish, but fell once more to studying the incomprehensible prospect.

Their view was towards the east, but over the river and the reaches of what had once upon a time been Long Island City and

16

Brooklyn, as familiar a scene in the other days as could be possibly imagined. But now how altered an aspect greeted them!

"It's surely all wiped out, all gone, gone into ruins," said Stern slowly and carefully, weighing each word. "No hallucination about that." He swept the sky-line with his eyes, that now peered keenly out from beneath those bushy brows. Instinctively he brought his hand up to his breast. He started with surprise.

"What's this?" he cried. "Why, I -- I've got a full yard of whiskers. My good Lord! Whiskers on me? And I used to say -- "

He burst out laughing. At his beard he plucked with merriment that jangled horribly on the girl's tense nerves. Suddenly he grew serious. For the first time he seemed to take clear notice of his companion's plight.

"Why, what a time it must have been!" cried he. "Here's some calculation all cut out for me, all right. But -- you can't go that way, Miss Kendrick. It -- it won't do, you know. Got to have something to put on. Great Heavens what a situation!"

He tried to peel off his remnant of a coat, but at the merest touch it tore to shreds and fell away. The girl restrained him.

"Never mind," said she, with quiet, modest dignity. "My hair protects me very well for the present. If you and I are all that's left of the people in the world, this is no time for trifles."

A moment he studied her. Then he nodded, and grew very grave.

"Forgive me," he whispered, laying a hand on her shoulder. Once more he turned to the window and looked out.

"So then, it's all gone?" he queried, speaking as to himself. "Only a skyscraper standing here or there? And the bridges and the islands -- all changed.

"Not a sign of life anywhere; not a sound; the forests growing thick among the ruins? A dead world if -- if all the world is like this part of it! All dead, save you and me!"

In silence they stood there, striving to realize the full import of the catastrophe. And Stern, deep down in his heart, caught some glimmering insight of the future and was glad.

3. On the Tower Platform

Suddenly the girl started, rebelling against the evidence of her own senses, striving again to force upon herself the belief that, after all, it could not be so.

"No, no, no!" she cried. "This can't be true. It mustn't be. There's a mistake somewhere. This simply must be all an illusion, a dream!

"If the whole world's dead, how does it happen we're alive? How do we know it's dead? Can we see it all from here? Why, all we see is just a little segment of things. Perhaps if we could know the truth, look farther, and know -- "

He shook his head.

"I guess you'll find it's real enough," he answered, "no matter how far you look. But, just the same, it won't do any harm to extend our radius of observation.

"Come, let's go on up to the top of the tower, up to the observation-platform. The quicker we know all the available facts the better. Now, if I only had a telescope -- !"

He thought hard a moment, then turned and strode over to a heap of friable disintegration that lay where once his instrument case had stood, containing his surveying tools.

Down on his ragged knees he fell; his rotten shreds of clothing tore and ripped at every movement, like so much water-soaked paper.

A strange, hairy, dust-covered figure, he knelt there. Quickly he plunged his hands into the rubbish and began pawing it over and over with eager haste.

"Ah!" he cried with triumph. "Thank Heaven, brass and lenses haven't crumbled yet!"

Up he stood again. In his hand the girl saw a peculiar telescope.

"My 'level,' see?" he exclaimed, holding it up to view. "The wooden tripod's long since gone. The fixtures that held it on won't bother me much.

"Neither will the spirit-glass on top. The main thing is that the telescope itself seems to be still intact. Now we'll see."

Speaking, he dusted off the eye-piece and the objective with a bit of rag from his coat-sleeve.

Beatrice noted that the brass tubes were all eaten and pitted with verdigris, but they still held firmly. And the lenses, when Stern had finished cleaning them, showed as bright and clear as ever.

"Come, now; come with me," he bade.

Out through the doorway into the hall he made his way while the girl followed. As she went she gathered her wondrous veil of hair more closely about her.

In this universal disorganization, this wreck of all the world, how little the conventions counted!

Together, picking their way up the broken stairs, where now the rust-bitten steel showed through the corroded stone and cement in a thousand places, they cautiously climbed.

Here, spider-webs thickly shrouded the way, and had to be brushed down. There, still more bats bung and chippered in protest as the intruders passed.

A fluffy little white owl blinked at them from a dark niche; and, well toward the top of the climb, they flushed up a score of mud-swallows which had ensconced themselves comfortably along a broken balustrade.

At last, however, despite all unforeseen incidents of this sort, they reached the upper platform, nearly a thousand feet above the earth.

Out through the relics of the revolving door they crept, he leading, testing each foot of the way before the girl. They reached the narrow platform of red tiling that surrounded the tower.

Even here they saw with growing amazement that the hand of time and of this maddening mystery had laid its heavy imprint.

"Look!" he exclaimed, pointing. "What this all means we don't know yet. How long it's been we can't tell. But to judge by the appearance up here, it's even longer than I thought. See, the very tiles are cracked and crumbling.

"Tilework is usually considered highly recalcitrant -- but this is gone. There's grass growing in the dust that's settled between the tiles. And -- why, here's a young oak that's taken root and forced a dozen slabs out of place."

"The winds and birds have carried seeds up here, and acorns," she answered in an awed voice. "Think of the time that must have passed. Years and years.

"But tell me," and her brow wrinkled with a sudden wonder, "tell me how we've ever lived so long? I can't understand it.

"Not only have we escaped starvation, but we haven't frozen to death in all these bitter winters. How can that have happened?"

"Let it all go as suspended animation till we learn the facts, if we ever do," he replied, glancing about with wonder.

"You know, of course, how toads have been known to live embedded in rock for centuries? How fish, hard-frozen, have been brought to life again? Well -- "

"But we are human beings."

"I know. Certain unknown natural forces, however, might have made no more of us than of non-mammalian and less highly organized creatures.

"Don't bother your head about these problems yet a while. On my word, we've got enough to do for the present without much caring about how or why.

"All we definitely know is that some very long, undetermined period of time has passed, leaving us still alive. The rest can wait."

"How long a time do you judge it?" she anxiously inquired.

"Impossible to say at once. But it must have been something extraordinary -- probably far longer than either of us suspect.

"See, for example, the attrition of everything up here exposed to the weather." He pointed at the heavy stone railing. "See how that is wrecked, for instance."

A whole segment, indeed, had fallen inward. Its débris lay in confusion, blocking all the southern side of the platform.

The bronze bars, which Stern well remembered -- two at each

corner, slanting downward and bracing a rail -- had now wasted to mere pockmarked shells of metal.

Three had broken entirely and sagged wantonly awry with the displacement of the stone blocks, between which the vines and grasses had long been carrying on their destructive work.

"Look out!" Stern cautioned. "Don't lean against any of those stones." Firmly he held her back as she, eagerly inquisitive, started to advance toward the railing.

"Don't go anywhere near the edge. It may all be rotten and undermined, for anything we know. Keep back here, close to the wall."

Sharply he inspected it a moment.

"Facing stones are pretty well gone," said he, "but, so far as I can see, the steel frame isn't too bad. Putting everything together, I'll probably be able before long to make some sort of calculation of the date. But for now we'll have to call it 'X,' and let it go at that."

"The year X!" she whispered under her breath. "Good Heavens, am I as old as that?"

He made no answer, but only drew her to him protectingly, while all about them the warm summer wind swept onward to the sea, out over the sparkling expanses of the bay -- alone unchanged in all that universal wreckage.

In the breeze her heavy masses of hair stirred luringly. He felt its silken caress on his half-naked shoulder, and in his ears the blood began to pound with strange insistence.

Quite gone now the daze and drowsiness of the first wakening. Stern did not even feel weak or shaken. On the contrary, never had life bounded more warmly, more fully, in his veins.

The presence of the girl set his heart throbbing heavily, but he bit his lip and restrained every untoward thought.

Only his arm tightened a little about that warmly clinging body. Beatrice did not shrink from him. She needed his protection as never since the world began had woman needed man.

To her it seemed that come what might, his strength and comfort could not fail. And, despite everything, she could not -- for the moment -- find unhappiness within her heart.

21

Quite vanished now, even in those brief minutes since their awakening, was all consciousness of their former relationship -- employer and employed.

The self-contained, courteous, yet unapproachable engineer had disappeared.

Now, through all the extraneous disguise of his outer self, there lived and breathed just a man, a young man, thewed with the vigor of his plentitude. All else had been swept clean away by this great change.

The girl was different, too. Was this strong woman, eager-eyed and brave, the quiet, low-voiced stenographer he remembered, busy only with her machine, her file-boxes, and her carbon-copies? Stern dared not realize the transmutation. He ventured hardly fringe it in his thoughts.

To divert his wonderings and to ease a situation which oppressed him, he began adjusting the "level" telescope to his eye.

With his back planted firmly against the tower, he studied a wide section of the dead and buried world so very far below them. With astonishment he cried:

"It is true, Beatrice! Everything's swept clean away. Nothing left, nothing at all -- no signs of life!

"As far as I can reach with these lenses, universal ruin. We're all alone in this whole world, just you and I -- and everything belongs to us!"

"Everything -- all ours?"

"Everything! Even the future -- the future of the human race!"

Suddenly he felt her tremble at his side. Down at her he looked, a great new tenderness possessing him. He saw that tears were forming in her eyes.

Beatrice pressed both hands to her face and bowed her head. Filled with strange emotions, the man watched her for a moment.

Then in silence, realizing the uselessness of any words, knowing that in this monstrous Ragnarok of all humanity no ordinary relations of life could bear either cogency or meaning, he took her in his arms.

And there alone with her, far above the ruined world, high in the pure air of mid-heaven, he comforted the girl with words till then unthought-of and unknown to him.

4. The City of Death

Presently Beatrice grew calmer. For though grief and terror still weighed upon her soul, she realized that this was no fit time to yield to any weakness -- now when a thousand things were pressing for accomplishment, if their own lives, too, were not presently to be snuffed out in all this universal death.

"Come, come," said Stern reassuringly. "I want you, too, to get a complete idea of what has happened. From now on you must know all, share all, with me." And, taking her by the hand he led her along the crumbling and uncertain platform.

Together, very cautiously, they explored the three sides of the platform still unchoked by ruins.

Out over the incredible mausoleum of civilization they peered. Now and again they fortified their vision by recourse to the telescope.

Nowhere, as he had said, was any slightest sign of life to be discerned. Nowhere a thread of smoke arose; nowhere a sound echoed upward.

Dead lay the city, between its rivers, whereon now no sail glinted in the sunlight, no tug puffed vehemently with plumy jets of steam, no liner idled at anchor or nosed its slow course out to sea.

The Jersey shore, the Palisades, the Bronx and Long Island all lay buried in dense forests of conifers and oak, with only here and there some skeleton mockery of a steel structure jutting through.

The islands in the harbor, too, were thickly overgrown. On Ellis, no sign of the immigrant station remained. Castle William was quite gone. And with a gasp of dismay and pain, Beatrice pointed out the fact that no longer Liberty held her bronze torch aloft.

Save for a black, misshapen mass protruding through the tree-tops, the huge gift of France was no more.

Fringing the water-front, all the way round, the mournful remains of the docks and piers lay in a mere sodden jumble of decay, with an occasional hulk sunk alongside.

Even over these wrecks of liners, vegetation was growing rank and green. All the wooden ships, barges and schooners had utterly vanished.

The telescope showed only a stray, lolling mast of steel, here or yonder, thrusting up from the desolation, like a mute appealing hand raised to a Heaven that responded not.

"See," remarked Stern, "up-town almost all the buildings seem to have crumbled in upon themselves, or to have fallen outward into the streets. What an inconceivable tangle of detritus those streets must be!

"And, do you notice the park hardly shows at all? Everything's so overgrown with trees you can't tell where it begins or ends. Nature has her revenge at last, on man!"

"The universal claim, made real," said Beatrice. "Those rather clearer lines of green, I suppose, must be the larger streets. See how the avenues stretch away and away, like ribbons of green velvet?"

"Everywhere that roots can hold at all, Mother Nature has set up her flags again. Hark! What's that?"

For a moment they listened intently. Up to them, from very far, rose a wailing cry, tremulous, long-drawn, formidable.

"Oh! Then there are people, after all?" faltered the girl, grasping Stern's arm.

He laughed.

"No, hardly!" answered he. "I see you don't know the wolf-cry. I didn't till I heard it in the Hudson Bay country, last winter -- that is, last winter, plus X. Not very pleasant, is it?"

"Wolves! Then -- there are -- "

"Why not? Probably all sorts of game on the island now. Why shouldn't there be? All in Mother Nature's stock-in-trade, you know.

"But come, come, don't let that worry you. We're safe, for the present. Time enough to consider hunting later. Let's creep around here to the other side of the tower, and see what we can see."

Silently she acquiesced. Together they reached the southern

25

part of the platform, making their way as far as the jumbled rocks of the fallen railing would permit.

Very carefully they progressed, fearful every moment lest the support break beneath them and hurl them down along the sloping side of the pinnacle to death.

"Look!" bade Stern, pointing. "That very long green line there used to be Broadway. Quite a respectable Forest of Arden now, isn't it?" He swept his hand far outward.

"See those steel cages, those tiny, far-off ones with daylight shining through? You know them -- the Park Row, the Singer, the Woolworth and all the rest. And the bridges, look at those!"

She shivered at the desolate sight. Of the Brooklyn Bridge only the towers were visible.

The watchers, two isolated castaways on their island in the sea of uttermost desolation, beheld a dragging mass of wreckage that drooped from these towers on either shore, down to the sparkling flood.

The other bridges, newer and stronger far, still remained standing. But even from that distance Stern could quite plainly see, without the telescope, that the Williamsburg Bridge had "buckled" downward and that the farther span of the Blackwell's Island Bridge was in ruinous disrepair.

"How horrible, how ghastly is all this waste and ruin!" thought the engineer. "Yet, even in their overthrow, how wonderful are the works of man!"

A vast wonder seized him as he stood there gazing; a fierce desire to rehabilitate all this wreckage, to set it right, to start the wheels of the world-machinery running once more.

At the thought of his own powerlessness a bitter smile curled his lips.

Beatrice seemed to share something of his wonder.

"Can it be possible," whispered she, "that you and -- and I -- are really like Macaulay's lone watcher of the world-wreck on London Bridge? That we are actually seeing the thing so often dreamed of by prophets and poets? That 'All this mighty heart is lying still,' at last -- forever? The heart of the world, never to beat again?"

He made no answer, save to shake his head; but fast his thoughts were running.

So then, could he and Beatrice, just they two, be in stern reality the sole survivors of the entire human race? That race for whose material welfare he had, once on a time, done such tremendous work?

Could they be destined, he and she, to witness the closing chapter in the long, painful, glorious Book of Evolution? Slightly he shivered and glanced round.

Till he could adjust his reason to the facts, could learn the truth and weigh it, he knew he must not analyze too closely; he felt he must try not to think. For that way lay madness!

Far out she gazed.

The sun, declining, shot a broad glory all across the sky. Purple and gold and crimson lay the light-bands over the breast of the Hudson.

Dark blue the shadows streamed across the ruined city with its crowding forests, its blank-staring windows and sagging walls, its thousands of gaping vacancies, where wood and stone and brick had crumbled down -- the city where once the tides of human life had ebbed and flowed, roaring resistlessly.

High overhead drifted a few rosy clouds, part of that changeless nature which alone did not repel or mystify these two beleaguered waifs, these chance survivors, this man, this woman, left alone together by the hand of fate.

They were dazed, fascinated by the splendor of that sunset over a world devoid of human life, for the moment giving up all efforts to judge or understand.

Stern and his mate peered closer, down at the interwoven jungles of Union Square, the leafy frond-masses that marked the one-time course of Twenty-Third Street, the forest in Madison Square, and the truncated column of the tower where no longer Diana turned her huntress bow to every varying breeze.

They heard their own hearts beat. The intake of their breath sounded strangely loud. Above them, on a broken cornice, some resting swallows twittered.

All at once the girl spoke.

"See the Flatiron Building over there!" said she. "What a hideous wreck!"

From Stern she took the telescope, adjusted it, and gazed minutely at the shattered pile of stone and metal.

Blotched as with leprosy stood the walls, whence many hundreds of blocks had fallen into Broadway forming a vast moraine that for some distance choked that thoroughfare.

In numberless places the steel frame peered through. The whole roof had caved in, crushing down the upper stories, of which only a few sparse upstanding metal beams remained.

The girl's gaze was directed at a certain spot which she knew well.

"Oh, I can even see into some of the offices on the eighteenth floor!" cried she. "There, look?" And she pointed. "That one near the front! I -- I used to know -- "

She broke short off. In her trembling hands the telescope sank. Stern saw that she was very pale.

"Take me down!" she whispered. "I can't stand it any longer, I can't possibly! The sight of that wrecked office! Let's go down where I can't see that!"

Gently, as though she had been a frightened child, Stern led her round the platform to the doorway, then down the crumbling stairs and so to the wreckage and dust-strewn confusion of what had been his office.

And there, his hand upon her shoulder, he bade her still be of good courage.

"Listen now, Beatrice," said he. "Let's try to reason this thing out together, let's try to solve this problem like two intelligent human beings.

"Just what's happened, we don't know; we can't know yet a while, till I investigate. We don't even know what year this is. Don't know whether anybody else is still alive, anywhere in the world. But we can find out -- after we've made provision for the immediate present and formed some rational plan of life. If all the rest are gone, swept away, wiped out clean like figures on a slate, then why we should have happened to survive whatever it was that struck the earth, is still a riddle far beyond our comprehension."

He raised her face to his, noble despite all its grotesque disfigurements; he looked into her eyes as though to read the very soul of her, to judge whether she could share this fight, could brave this coming struggle.

"All these things may yet be answered. Once I get the proper data for this series of phenomena, I can find the solution, never fear!

"Some vast world-duty may be ours, far greater, infinitely more vital than anything that either of us has ever dreamed. It's not our place, now, to mourn or fear! Rather it is to read this mystery, to meet it and to conquer!"

Through her tears the girl smiled up at him, trustingly, confidingly. And in the last declining rays of the sun that glinted through the window-pane, her eyes were very beautiful.

5. Exploration

Came now the evening, as they sat and talked together, talked long and earnestly, there within that ruined place. Too eager for some knowledge of the truth, they, to feel hunger or to think of their lack of clothing.

Chairs they had none, nor even so much as a broom to clean the floor with. But Stern, first-off, had wrenched a marble slab from the stairway.

And with this plank of stone still strong enough to serve, he had scraped all one corner of the office floor free of rubbish. This gave them a preliminary camping-place wherein to take their bearings and discuss what must be done.

"So then," the engineer was saying as the dusk grew deeper, "so then, we'll apparently have to make this building our headquarters for a while.

"As nearly as I can figure, this is about what must have happened. Some sudden, deadly, numbing plague or cataclysm must have struck the earth, long, long ago.

"It may have been an almost instantaneous onset of some new and highly fatal micro-organism, propagating with such marvelous rapidity that it swept the world clean in a day -- doing its work before any resistance could be organized or thought of.

"Again, some poisonous gas may have developed, either from a fissure in the earth's crust, or otherwise. Other hypotheses are possible, but of what practical value are they now?

"We only know that here, in this uppermost office of the Tower, you and I have somehow escaped with only a long period of completely suspended animation. How long? God alone knows! That's a query I can't even guess the answer to as yet."

"Well, to judge by all the changes," Beatrice suggested thoughtfully, "it can't have been less than a hundred years. Great Heavens!" and she burst into a little satiric laugh. "Am I a hundred and twenty-four years old? Think of that!"

"You underestimate," Stern answered. "But no matter about the time question for the present; we can't solve it now.

"Neither can we solve the other problem about Europe and Asia and all the rest of the world. Whether London, Paris, Berlin, Rome, and every other city, every other land, all have shared this fate, we simply don't know.

"All we can have is a feeling of strong probability that life, human life I mean, is everywhere extinct -- save right here in this room!

"Otherwise, don't you see, men would have made their way back here again, back to New York, where all these incalculable treasures seem to have perished, and -- "

He broke short off. Again, far off, they heard a faint re-echoing roar. For a moment they both sat speechless. What could it be? Some distant wall toppling down? A hungry beast scenting its prey? They could not tell. But Stern smiled.

"I guess," said he, "guns will be about the first thing I'll look for, after food. There ought to be good hunting down in the jungles of Fifth Avenue and Broadway!

"You shoot, of course? No? Well, I'll soon teach you. Lots of things both of us have got to learn now. No end of them!"

He rose from his place on the floor, went over to the window and stood for a minute peering out into the gloom. Then suddenly he turned.

"What's the matter with me, anyhow?" he exclaimed with irritation. "What right have I to be staying here, theorizing, when there's work to do? I ought to be busy this very minute!

"In some way or other I've got to find food, clothing, tools, arms -- a thousand things. And above all, water! And here I've been speculating about the past, fool that I am!"

"You -- you aren't going to leave me -- not to-night?" faltered the girl.

Stern seemed not to have heard her, so strong the imperative of action lay upon him now. He began to pace the floor, sliding and stumbling through the rubbish, a singular figure in his tatters and with his patriarchal hair and beard, a figure dimly seen by the faint light that still gloomed through the window.

"In all that wreckage down below," said he, as though half to himself, "in all that vast congeries of ruin which once was called New York, surely enough must still remain intact for our small needs. Enough till we can reach the land, the country, and raise food of our own!"

"Don't go now!" pleaded Beatrice. She, too, stood up, and out she stretched her hands to him. "Don't, please! We can get along some way or other till morning. At least, I can!"

"No, no, it isn't right! Down in the shops and stores, who knows but we might find -- "

"But you're unarmed! And in the streets -- in the forest, rather -- "

"Listen!" he commanded rather abruptly. "This is no time for hesitating or for weakness. I know you'll stand your share of all that we must suffer, dare and do together.

"Some way or other I've got to make you comfortable. I've got to locate food and drink immediately. Got to get my bearings. Why, do you think I'm going to let you, even for one night, go fasting and thirsty, sleep on bare cement, and all that sort of thing?

"If so, you're mistaken! No, you must spare me for an hour or two. Inside of that time I ought to make a beginning!"

"A whole hour?"

"Two would probably be nearer it. I promise to be back inside of that time."

"But," and her voice quivered just a trifle, "but suppose some wolf or bear -- "

"Oh, I'm not quite so foolhardy as all that!" he retorted. "I'm not going to venture outside till to-morrow. My idea is that I can find at least a few essentials right here in this building.

"It's a city in itself -- or was. Offices, stores, shops, everything right here together in a lump. It can't possibly take me very long to go down and rummage out something for your comfort.

"Now that the first shock and surprise of our awakening are over, we can't go on in this way, you know -- h'm! -- dressed in -- well, such exceedingly primitive garb!"

Silently she looked at his dim figure in the dusk. Then she stretched out her hand.

"I'll go too," said she quite simply.

"You'd better stay. It's safer here."

"No, I'm going."

"But if we run into dangers?"

"Never mind. Take me with you."

Over to her he came. He took her hand. In silence he pressed it. Thus for a moment they stood. Then, arousing himself to action, he said: "First of all, a light."

"A light? How can you make a light? Why, there isn't a match left anywhere in this whole world."

"I know, but there are other things. Probably my chemical flasks and vials aren't injured. Glass is practically imperishable. And if I'm not mistaken, the bottles must be lying somewhere in that rubbish heap over by the window."

He left her wondering, and knelt among the litter. For a while he silently delved through the triturated bits of punky wood and rust-red metal that now represented the remains of his chemical cabinet.

All at once he exclaimed: "Here's one! And here's another! This certainly is luck! H-m! I shouldn't wonder if I got almost all of them back."

One by one he found a score of thick, ground-glass vials. Some were broken, probably by the shock when they and the cabinet had fallen, but a good many still remained intact.

Among these were the two essential ones. By the last dim ghost of light through the window, and by the sense of touch, Stern was able to make out the engraved symbols "P" and "S" on these bottles.

"Phosphorus and sulphur," he commented. "Well, what more could I reasonably ask? Here's alcohol, too, hermetically sealed. Not too bad, eh?"

While the girl watched, with wondering admiration, Stern thought hard a moment. Then he set to work.

First he took a piece of the corroded metal framework of the cabinet, a steel strip about eighteen inches long, frail in places, but still sufficiently strong to serve his purpose.

Tearing off some rags from his coat-sleeve, he wadded them together into a ball as big as his fist. Around this ball he twisted the metal strip, so that it formed at once a holder and a handle for the rag-mass.

With considerable difficulty he worked the glass stopper out of the alcohol bottle, and with the fluid saturated the rags. Then, on a clear bit of the floor, he spilled out a small quantity of the phosphorus and sulphur.

"This beats getting fire by friction all hollow," he cheerfully remarked. "I've tried that, too, and I guess it's only in books a white man ever succeeds at it. But this way you see, it's simplicity itself."

Very moderate friction, with a bit of wood from the wreckage of the door, sufficed to set the phosphorus ablaze. Stern heaped on a few tiny lumps of sulphur. Then, coughing as the acrid fumes arose from the sputter of blue flame, he applied the alcohol-soaked torch.

Instantly a puff of fire shot up, colorless and clear, throwing no very satisfactory light, yet capable of dispelling the thickest of the gloom.

The blaze showed Stern's eager face, long-bearded and dusty, as he bent over this crucial experiment.

The girl, watching closely, felt a strange new thrill of confidence and solace. Some realization of the engineer's resourcefulness came to her, and in her heart she had confidence that, though the whole wide world had crumbled into ruin, yet he would find a way to smooth her path, to be a strength and refuge for her.

But Stern had no time for any but matters of intensest practicality. From the floor he arose, holding the flambeau in one hand, the bottle of alcohol in the other.

"Come now," bade he, and raised the torch on high to light her way, "You're still determined to go?"

For an answer she nodded. Her eyes gleamed by the uncanny light.

And so, together, he leading out of the room and along the wrecked hall, they started on their trip of exploration out into the unknown.

6. Treasure-Trove

Never before had either of them realized just what the meaning of forty-eight stories might be. For all their memories of this height were associated with smooth-sliding elevators that had whisked them up as though the tremendous height had been the merest trifle.

This night, however, what with the broken stairs, the débris-cumbered hallways, the lurking darkness which the torch could hardly hold back from swallowing them, they came to a clear understanding of the problem.

Every few minutes the flame burned low and Stern had to drop on more alcohol, holding the bottle high above the flame to avoid explosion.

Long before they had compassed the distance to the ground floor the girl lagged with weariness and shrank with nameless fears.

Each black doorway that yawned along their path seemed ominous with memories of life that had perished there, of death that now reigned all-supreme.

Each corner, every niche and crevice, breathed out the spirit of the past and of the mystic tragedy which in so brief a time had wiped the human race from earth, "as a mother wipes the milky lips of her child."

And Stern, though he said little save to guide Beatrice and warn her of unusual difficulties, felt the somber magic of the place. No poet, he; only a man of hard and practical details. Yet he realized that, were he dowered with the faculty, here lay matter for an Epic of Death such as no Homer ever dreamed, no Virgil ever could have penned.

Now and then, along the corridors and down the stairways, they chanced on curious little piles of dust, scattered at random in fantastic shapes.

These for a few minutes puzzled Stern, till stooping, he stirred one with his hand. Something he saw there made him start back with a stifled exclamation.

"What is it?" cried the girl, startled. "Tell me!"

But he, realizing the nature of his discovery -- for he had seen a human incisor tooth, gold-filled, there in the odd little heap -- straightened up quickly and assumed to smile.

"It's nothing, nothing at all!" he answered. "Come, we haven't got any time to waste. If we're going to provide ourselves with even a few necessaries before the alcohol's all gone, we've got to be at work!"

And onward, downward, ever farther and farther, he led her through the dark maze of ruin, which did not even echo to their barefoot tread.

Like disheveled wraiths they passed, soundlessly, through eerie labyrinths and ways which might have served as types of Coleridge's "caverns measureless to man," so utterly drear they stretched out in their ghostly desolation.

At length, after an eternal time of weariness and labor, they managed to make their way down into the ruins of the once famous and beautiful arcade which had formerly run from Madison Avenue to the square.

"Oh, how horrible!" gasped Beatrice, shrinking, as they clambered down the stairs and emerged into this scene of chaos, darkness, death.

Where long ago the arcade had stretched its path of light and life and beauty, of wealth and splendor, like an epitome of civilization all gathered in that constricted space, the little light disclosed stark horror.

Feeble as a will-o'-the-wisp in that enshrouding dark, the torch showed only hints of things -- here a fallen pillar, there a shattered mass of wreckage where a huge section of the ceiling had fallen, yonder a gaping aperture left by the disintegration of a wall.

Through all this rubbish and confusion, over and through a score of the little dust-piles which Stern had so carefully avoided explaining to Beatrice, they climbed and waded, and with infinite pains slowly advanced.

"What we need is more light!" exclaimed the engineer presently. "We've got to have a bonfire here!"

And before long he had collected a considerable pile of wood, ripped from the door-ways and window-casings of the arcade. This he set fire to, in the middle of the floor.

Soon a dull, wavering glow began to paint itself upon the walls, and to fling the comrades' shadows, huge and weird, in dancing mockery across the desolation.

Strangely enough, many of the large plate-glass windows lining the arcade still stood intact. They glittered with the uncanny reflections of the fire as the man and woman slowly made way down the passage.

"See," exclaimed Stern, pointing. "See all these ruined shops? Probably almost everything is worthless. But there must be some things left that we can use.

"See the post-office, down there on the left? Think of the millions in real money, gold and silver, in all these safes here and all over the city -- in the banks and vaults! Millions! Billions!

"Jewels, diamonds, wealth simply inconceivable! Yet now a good water supply, some bread, meat, coffee, salt, and so on, a couple of beds, a gun or two and some ordinary tools would outweigh them all!"

"Clothes, too," the girl suggested. "Plain cotton cloth is worth ten million dollars an inch now."

"Right," answered Stern, gazing about him with wonder.

"And I offer a bushel of diamonds for a razor and a pair of scissors." Grimly he smiled as he stroked his enormous beard.

"But come, this won't do. There'll be plenty of time to look around and discuss things in the morning. Just now we've got a definite errand. Let's get busy!"

Thus began their search for a few prime necessities of life, there in that charnel-house of civilization, by the dull reflections of the firelight and the pallid torch glow.

Though they forced their way into ten or twelve of the arcade shops, they found no clothing, no blankets or fabric of any kind that would serve for coverings or to sleep upon. Everything at all in the nature of cloth had either sunk back into moldering annihilation or had at best grown far too fragile to be of the slightest service.

They found, however, a furrier's shop, and this they entered eagerly.

From rusted metal hooks a few warped fragments of skins still hung, moth-eaten, riddled with holes, ready to crumble at the merest touch.

"There's nothing in any of these to help us," judged Stern. "But maybe we might find something else in here."

Carefully they searched the littered place, all dust and horrible disarray, which made sad mockery of the gold-leaf sign still visible on the window: "Lange, Importer. All the Latest Novelties."

On the floor Stern discovered three more of those little dust-middens which meant human bodies, pitiful remnants of an extinct race, of unknown people in the long ago. What had he now in common with them? The remains did not even inspire repugnance in him. All at once Beatrice uttered a cry of startled gladness. "Look here! A storage chest!"

True enough, there stood a cedar box, all seamed and cracked and bulging, yet still retaining a semblance of its original shape.

The copper bindings and the lock were still quite plainly to be seen, as the engineer held the torch close, though green and corroded with incredible age.

One effort of Stern's powerful arms sufficed to tip the chest quite over. As it fell it burst. Down in a mass of pulverized, worm-eaten splinters it disintegrated.

Out rolled furs, many and many of them, black, and yellow, and striped -- the pelts of the grizzly, of the leopard, the chetah, the royal Bengal himself.

"Hurray!" shouted the man, catching up first one, then another, and still a third. "Almost intact. A little imperfection here and there doesn't matter. Now we've got clothes and beds.

"What's that? Yes, maybe they are a trifle warm for this season of the year, but this is no time to be particular. See, now, how do you like that?"

Over the girl's shoulders, as he spoke, he flung the tiger-skin.

"Magnificent!" he judged, standing back a pace or two and holding up the torch to see her better. "When I find you a big gold pin or clasp to fasten that with at the throat you'll make a picture of another and more splendid Boadicea!"

He tried to laugh at his own words, but merriment sat ill there in that place, and with such a subject. For the woman, thus clad, had suddenly assumed a wild, barbaric beauty.

Bright gleamed her gray eyes by the light of the flambeau; limpid, and deep, and earnest, they looked at Stern. Her wonderful hair, shaken out in bewildering masses over the striped, tawny savagery of the robe, made colorful contrasts, barbarous, seductive.

Half hidden, the woman's perfect body, beautiful as that of a wood-nymph or a pagan dryad, roused atavistic passions in the engineer.

He dared speak no other word for the moment, but bent beside the shattered chest again and fell to looking over the furs.

A polar-bear skin attracted his attention, and this he chose. Then, with it slung across his shoulder, he stood up.

"Come," said he, steadying his voice with an effort; "come, we must be going now. Our light won't hold out very much longer. We've got to find food and drink before the alcohol's all gone; got to look out for practical affairs, whatever happens. Let's be going."

Fortune favored them.

In the wreck of a small fancy grocer's booth down toward the end of the arcade, where the post-office had been, they came upon a stock of goods in glass jars.

All the tinned foods had long since perished, but the impermeable glass seemed to have preserved fruits and vegetables of the finer sort, and chipped beef and the like, in a state of perfect soundness.

Best of all, they discovered the remains of a case of mineral water. The case had crumbled to dust, but fourteen bottles of water were still intact.

"Pile three or four of these into my fur robe here," directed Stern. "Now, a few of the other jars -- that's right. Tomorrow we'll come down and clean up the whole stock. But we've got enough for now."

"We'd best be getting back up the stairs again," said he. And so they started.

"Are you going to leave that fire burning?" asked the girl, as they passed the middle of the arcade.

"Yes. It can't do any harm. Nothing to catch here; only old metal and cement. Besides, it would take too much time and labor to put it out."

Thus they abandoned the gruesome place and began the long, exhausting climb.

It must have taken them an hour and a half at least to reach their eerie. Both found their strength taxed to the utmost.

Before they were much more than halfway up, the ultimate drop of alcohol had been burned.

The last few hundred feet had to be made by slow, laborious feeling, aided only by such dim reflections of the gibbous moon as glimmered through a window, cobweb-hung, or through some break in the walls.

At length, however -- for all things have an end -- breathless and spent, they found their refuge. And soon after that, clad in their savage robes, they supped.

Allan Stern, consulting engineer, and Beatrice Kendrick, stenographer, now king and queen of the whole wide world domain (as they feared), sat together by a little blaze of punky wood fragments that flickered on the eroded floor.

They ate with their fingers and drank out of the bottles, sans apology. Strange were their speculations, their wonderings, their plans -- now discussed specifically, now half-voiced by a mere word that thrilled them both with sudden, poignant emotion.

An so an hour passed, and the night deepened toward the birth of another day. The fire burned low and died, for they had little to replenish it with.

Down sank the moon, her pale light dimming as she went, her

faint illumination wanly creeping across the disordered, wrack-strewn floor.

And at length Stern, in the outer office, Beatrice in the other, they wrapped themselves within their furs and laid them down to sleep.

Despite the age-long trance from which they both had but so recently emerged, a strange lassitude weighed on them.

Yet long after Beatrice had lost herself in dreams, Stern lay and thought strange thoughts, yearning and eager thoughts, there in the impenetrable gloom.

7. The Outer World

Before daybreak the engineer was up again, and active. Now that he faced the light of morning, with a thousand difficult problems closing in on every hand, he put aside his softer moods, his visions and desires, and -- like the scientific man he was -- addressed himself to the urgent matters in hand.

"The girl's safe enough alone, here, for a while," thought he, looking in upon her where she lay, calm as a child, folded within the clinging masses of the tiger-skin.

"I must be out and away for two or three hours, at the very least. I hope she'll sleep till I get back. If not -- what then?"

He thought a moment; then, coming over to the charred remnants of last night's fire, chose a bit of burnt wood. With this he scrawled in large, rough letters on a fairly smooth stretch of the wall:

Back soon. All O. K. Don't worry.

Then, turning, he set out on the long, painful descent again to the earth-level.

Garish now, and doubly terrible, since seen with more than double clearness by the graying dawn, the world-ruin seemed to him.

Strong of body and of nerve as he was, he could not help but shudder at the numberless traces of sudden and pitiless death which met his gaze.

Everywhere lay those dust-heaps, with here or there a tooth, a ring, a bit of jewelry showing -- everywhere he saw them, all the way down the stairs, in every room and office he peered into, and in the time-ravished confusion of the arcade.

But this was scarcely the time for reflections of any sort. Life called, and labor, and duty; not mourning for the dead world, nor even wonder or pity at the tragedy which had so mysteriously befallen.

And as the man made his way over and through the universal wreckage, he took counsel with himself.

"First of all, water!" thought he. "We can't depend on the bottled supply. Of course, there's the Hudson; but it's brackish, if not downright salt. I've got to find some fresh and pure supply, close at hand. That's the prime necessity of life.

"What with the canned stuff, and such game as I can kill, there's bound to be food enough for a while. But a good water-supply we must have, and at once!"

Yet, prudent rather for the sake of Beatrice than for his own, he decided that he ought not to issue out, unarmed, into this new and savage world, of which he had as yet no very definite knowledge. And for a while he searched hoping to find some weapon or other.

"I've got to have an ax, first of all," said he. "That's mans first need, in any wilderness. Where shall I find one?"

He thought a moment.

"Ah! In the basements!" exclaimed he. "Maybe I can locate an engine-room, a store-room, or something of that sort. There's sure to be tools in a place like that." And, laying off the bear-skin, he prepared to explore the regions under the ground-level.

He used more than half an hour, through devious ways and hard labor, to make his way to the desired spot. The ancient stairway, leading down, he could not find.

But by clambering down one of the elevator-shafts, digging toes and fingers into the crevices in the metal framework and the cracks in the concrete, he managed at last to reach a vaulted subcellar, festooned with webs, damp, noisome and obscure.

Considerable light glimmered in from a broken sidewalk-grating above, and through a gaping, jagged hole near one end of the cellar, beneath which lay a badly-broken stone.

The engineer figured that this block had fallen from the tower and come to rest only here; and this awoke him to a new sense of ever-present peril. At any moment of the night or day, he realized, some such mishap was imminent.

"Eternal vigilance!" he whispered to himself. Then, dismissing useless fears, he set about the task in hand.

By the dim illumination from above, he was able to take cognizance of the musty-smelling place, which, on the whole, was in a better state of repair than the arcade. The first cellar yielded nothing of value to him, but, making his way through a low vaulted door, he chanced into what must have been one of the smaller, auxiliary engine-rooms.

This, he found, contained a battery of four dynamos, a small seepage-pump, and a crumbling marble switch-board with part of the wiring still comparatively intact.

At sight of all this valuable machinery scaled and pitted with rust, Stern's brows contracted with a feeling akin to pain. The engineer loved mechanism of all sorts; its care and use had been his life.

And now these mournful relics, strange as that may seem, affected him more strongly than the little heaps of dust which marked the spots where human beings had fallen in sudden, inescapable death.

Yet even so, he had no time for musing.

"Tools!" cried he, peering about the dim lit vault. "Tools -- I must have some. Till I find tools, I'm helpless!"

Search as he might, he discovered no ax in the place, but in place of it he unearthed a sledge-hammer. Though corroded, it was still quite serviceable. Oddly enough, the oak handle was almost intact.

"Kyanized wood, probably," reflected he, as he laid the sledge to one side and began delving into a bed of dust that had evidently been a work-bench. "Ah! And here's a chisel! A spanner, too! A heap of rusty old wire nails!"

Delightedly he examined these treasures.

"They're worth more to me," he exulted; "than all the gold between here and what's left of San Francisco!"

He found nothing more of value in the litter. Everything else was rusted beyond use. So, having convinced himself that nothing more remained, he gathered up his finds and started back whence he had come.

After some quarter-hour of hard labor, he managed to transport everything up into the arcade.

"Now for a glimpse of the outer world!" quoth he.

Gripping the sledge well in hand, he made his way through the confused nexus of ruin. Disguised as everything now was, fallen and disjointed, murdering, blighted by age incalculable, still the man recognized many familiar features.

Here, he recalled, the telephone-booths had been; there the information desk. Yonder, again, he remembered the little curved counter where once upon a time a man in uniform had sold tickets to such as had wanted to visit the tower.

The counter now was dust; the ticket-man only a crumble of fine, grayish powder. Stern shivered slightly, and pressed on.

As he approached the outer air, he noticed that many a grassy tuft and creeping vine had rooted in the pavement of the arcade, up-prying the marble slabs and cracking the once magnificent floor.

The doorway itself was almost choked by a tremendous Norway pine which had struck root close to the building, and now insolently blocked that way where, other-time many thousand men and women every day had come and gone.

But Stern clambered out past this obstacle, testing the floor with his sledge, as he went, lest he fall through any unseen weak spots into the depths of coal-cellars below. And presently he reached the outer air, unharmed.

"But -- but, the sidewalk?" cried he, amazed. "The street -- the Square? Where are they?" And in astonishment he stopped, staring.

The view from the tower, though it had told him something of the changes wrought, had given him no adequate conception of their magnitude.

He had expected some remains of human life to show upon the earth, some semblance of the metropolis to remain in the street. But no, nothing was there; nothing at all on the ground to show that he was in the heart of a city.

He could, indeed, catch glimpses of a building here or there. Through the tangled thickets that grew close up to the age-worn walls of the Metropolitan, he could make out a few bits of tottering construction on the south side of what had been Twenty-Third Street.

But of the street itself, no trace remained -- no pavement, no sidewalk, no curb. And even so near and so conspicuous an object as the wreck of the Flatiron was now entirely concealed by the dense forest.

Soil had formed thickly over all the surface. Huge oaks and pines flourished there as confidently as though in the heart of the Maine forest, crowding ash and beech for room.

Under the man's feet, even as he stood close by the building -- which was thickly overgrown with ivy and with ferns and bushes rooted in the crannies -- the pine-needles bent in deep, pungent beds.

Birch, maple, poplar and all the natives of the American woods shouldered each other lustily. By the state of the fresh young leaves, just bursting their sheaths, Stern knew the season was mid-May.

Through the wind-swayed branches, little flickering patches of morning sunlight met his gaze, as they played and quivered on the forest moss or over the sere pine-spills.

Even upon the huge, squared stones which here and there lay in disorder, and which Stern knew must have fallen from the tower, the moss grew very thick; and more than one such block had been rent by frost and growing things.

"How long has it been, great Heavens! How long?" cried the engineer, a sudden fear creeping into his heart. For this, the reasserted dominance of nature, bore in on him with more appalling force than anything he had yet seen.

About him he looked, trying to get his bearings in that strange milieu.

"Why," said he, quite slowly, "it's -- it's just as though some cosmic jester, all-powerful, had scooped up the fragments of a ruined city and tossed them pell-mell into the core of the Adirondacks! It's horrible -- ghastly -- incredible!"

Dazed and awed, he stood as in a dream, a strange figure with his mane of hair, his flaming, trailing beard, his rags (for he had left the bear-skin in the arcade), his muscular arm, knotted as he held the sledge over his shoulder.

Well might he have been a savage of old times; one of the early barbarians of Britain, perhaps, peering in wonder at the ruins of some deserted Roman camp.

The chatter of a squirrel high up somewhere in the branches of an oak, recalled him to his wits. Down came spiralling a few bits of bark and acorn-shell, quite in the old familiar way.

Farther off among the woods, a robin's throaty morning notes drifted to him on the odorous breeze. A wren, surprisingly tame, chippered busily. It hopped about, not ten feet from him, entirely fearless.

Stern realized that it was now seeing a man for the first time in its life, and that it had no fear. His bushy brows contracted as he watched the little brown body jumping from twig to twig in the pine above him.

A deep, full breath he drew. Higher, still higher he raised his head. Far through the leafy screen he saw the overbending arch of sky in tiny patches of turquoise.

"The same old world, after all -- the same, in spite of everything -- thank God!" he whispered, his very tone a prayer of thanks.

And suddenly, though why he could not have told, the grim engineer's eyes grew wet with tears that ran, unheeded, down his heavy-bearded cheeks.

8. A Sign of Peril

Stern's weakness -- as he judged it -- lasted but a minute. Then, realizing even more fully than ever the necessity for immediate labor and exploration, he tightened his grip upon the sledge and set forth into the forest of Madison Square.

Away from him scurried a cotton-tail. A snake slid, hissing, out of sight under a jungle of fern. A butterfly, dull brown and ocher, settled upon a branch in the sunlight, where it began slowly opening and shutting its wings.

"Hem! That's a Danaus plexippus, right enough," commented the man. "But there are some odd changes in it. Yes, indeed, certainly some evolutionary variants. Must be a tremendous time since we went to sleep, for sure; probably very much longer than I dare guess. That's a problem I've got to go to work on, before many days!"

But now for the present he dismissed it again; he pushed it aside in the press of urgent matters. And, parting the undergrowth, he broke his crackling way through the deep wood.

He had gone but a few hundred yards when an exclamation of surprised delight burst from his lips.

"Water! Water!" he cried. "What? A spring, so close? A pool, right here at hand? Good luck, by Jove, the very first thing!"

And, stopping where he stood, he gazed at it with keen, unalloyed pleasure.

There, so near to the massive bulk of the tower that the vast shadow lay broadly across it, Stern had suddenly come upon as beautiful a little watercourse as ever bubbled forth under the yews of Arden or lapped the willows of Hesperides.

He beheld a roughly circular depression in the woods, fern-banked and fringed with purple blooms; at the bottom sparkled a spring, leaf-bowered, cool, Elysian.

49

From this, down through a channel which the water must have worn for itself by slow erosion, a small brook trickled, widening out into a pool some fifteen feet across; whence, brimming over, it purled away through the young sweet-flags and rushes with tempting little woodland notes.

"What a find!" cried the engineer. Forward he strode. "So, then? Deer-tracks?" he exclaimed, noting a few dainty hoof-prints in the sandy margin. "Great!" And, filled with exultation, he dropped beside the spring.

Over it he bent. Setting his bearded lips to the sweet water, he drank enormous, satisfying drafts.

Sated at last, he stood up again and peered about him. All at once he burst out into joyous laughter.

"Why, this is certainly an old friend of mine, or I'm a liar!" he cried out. "This spring is nothing more or less than the lineal descendant of Madison Square fountain, what? But good Lord, what a change!

"It would make a splendid subject for an article in the *Annals of Applied Geology*. Only -- well, there aren't any annals, now, and what's more, no readers!"

Down to the wider pool he walked.

"Stern, my boy," said he, "here's where you get an A-1, first-class dip!"

A minute later, stripped to the buff, the man lay splashing vigorously in the water. From top to toe he scrubbed himself vigorously with the fine, white sand. And when, some minutes later, he rose up again, the tingle and joy of life filled him in every nerve.

For a minute he looked contemptuously at his rags, lying there on the edge of the pool. Then with a grunt he kicked them aside.

"I guess we'll dispense with those," judged he. "The bear-skin, back in the building, there, will be enough." He picked up his sledge, and, heaving a mighty breath of comfort, set out for the tower again.

"Ah, but that was certainly fine!" he exclaimed. "I feel ten years younger, already. Ten, from what? X minus ten, equals -- ?"

Thoughtfully, as he walked across the elastic moss and over the pine-needles, he stroked his beard.

"Now, if I could only get a hair-cut and shave!" said he. "Well, why not? Wouldn't that surprise her, though?"

The idea strong upon him, he hastened his steps, and soon was back at the door close to the huge Norway pine. But here he did not enter. Instead, he turned to the right.

Plowing through the woods, climbing over fallen columns and shattered building-stones, flushing a covey of loud-winged partridges, parting the bushes that grew thickly along the base of the wall, he now found himself in what had long ago been Twenty-Third Street.

No sign, now of paving or car tracks -- nothing save, on the other side of the way, crumbling lines of ruin. As he worked his way among the detritus of the Metropolitan, he kept sharp watch for the wreckage of a hardware store.

Not until he had crossed the ancient line of Madison Avenue and penetrated some hundred yards still further along Twenty-Third Street, did he find what he sought. "Ah!" he suddenly cried. "Here's something now!"

And, scrambling over a pile of grass-grown rubbish with a couple of time-bitten iron wheels peering out -- evidently the wreckage of an electric car -- he made his way around a gaping hole where a side-walk had caved in and so reached the interior of a shop.

"Yes, prospects here, certainly prospects!" he decided carefully inspecting the place. "If this didn't use to be Currier & Brown's place, I'm away off my bearings. There ought to be something left."

"Ah! Would you?" and he flung a hastily-snatched rock at a rattlesnake that had begun its dry, chirring defiance on top of what once had been a counter.

The snake vanished, while the rock rebounding, crashed through glass.

Stern wheeled about with a cry of joy. For there, he saw, still stood near the back of the shop a showcase from within which he caught a sheen of tarnished metal.

Quickly he ran toward this, stumbling over the loose flooring, mossy and grass-grown. There in the case, preserved as you have seen Egyptian relics two or three thousand years old, in museums, the engineer beheld incalculable treasures. He thrilled with a savage, strange delight.

Another blow, with the sledge, demolished the remaining glass.

He trembled with excitement as he chose what he most needed.

"I certainly do understand now," said he, "why the New Zealanders took Captain Cook's old barrel-hoops and refused his cash. Same here! All the money in this town couldn't buy this rusty knife -- " as he seized a corroded blade set in a horn handle, yellowed with age. And eagerly he continued the hunt.

Fifteen minutes later he had accumulated a pair of scissors, two rubber combs, another knife, a revolver, an automatic, several handfuls of cartridges and a Cosmos bottle.

All these he stowed in a warped, mildewed remnant of a Gladstone bag, taken from a corner where a broken glass sign, "Leather Goods," lay among the rank confusion.

"I guess I've got enough, now, for the first load," he judged, more excited than if he had chanced upon a blue-clay bed crammed with Cullinan diamonds. "It's a beginning, anyhow. Now for Beatrice!"

Joyously as a schoolboy with a pocketful of new-won marbles, he made his exit from the ruins of the hardware store, and started back toward the tower.

But hardly had he gone a hundred feet when all at once he drew back with a sharp cry of wonder and alarm.

There at his feet, in plain view under a little maple sapling, lay something that held him frozen with astonishment.

He snatched it up, dropping the sledge to do so.

"What? What?" he stammered; and at the thing he stared with widened, uncomprehending eyes.

"Merciful God! How -- what -- ?" cried he.

The thing he held in his hand was a broad, fat, flint assegai-point!

9. Headway Against Odds

Stern gazed at this alarming object with far more trepidation than he would have eyed a token authentically labeled: "Direct from Mars."

For the space of a full half-minute he found no word, grasped no coherent thought, came to no action save to stand there, thunder-struck, holding the rotten leather bag in one hand, the spearhead in the other.

Then, suddenly, he shouted a curse and made as though to fling it clean away. But ere it had left his grasp, he checked himself.

"No, there's no use in that," said he, quite slowly. "If this thing is what it appears to be, if it isn't merely some freakish bit of stone weathered off somewhere, why, it means -- my God, what doesn't it mean?"

He shuddered, and glanced fearfully about him; all his calculations already seemed crashing down about him; all his plans, half-formulated, appeared in ruin.

New, vast and unknown factors of the struggle broadened rapidly before his mental vision, if this thing were really what it looked to be.

Keenly he peered at the bit of flint in his palm. There it lay, real enough, an almost perfect specimen of the flaker's art, showing distinctly where the wood had been applied to the core to peel off the many successive layers.

It could not have been above three and a half inches long, by one and a quarter wide, at its broadest part. The heft, where it had been hollowed to hold the lashings, was well marked.

A diminutive object and a skilfully-formed one. At any other time or place, the engineer would have considered the finding a good fortune; but now -- !

"Yet after all," he said aloud, as if to convince himself, "it's only a bit of stone! What can it prove?"

His subconsciousness seemed to make answer: "So, too, the sign that Robinson Crusoe found on the beach was only a human foot-mark. Do not deceive yourself!"

In deep thought the engineer stood there a moment or two. Then, "Bah!" cried he. "What does it matter, anyhow? Let it come -- whatever it is! If I hadn't just happened to find this, I'd have been none the wiser." And he dropped the bit of flint into the bag along with the other things.

Again he picked up his sledge, and, now more cautiously, once more started forward.

"All I can do," he thought, "is just to go right ahead as though this hadn't happened at all. If trouble comes, it comes, that's all. I guess I can meet it. Always have got away with it, so far. We'll see. What's on the cards has got to be played to a finish, and the best hand wins!"

He retraced his way to the spring, where he carefully rinsed and filled the Cosmos bottle for Beatrice. Then back to the Metropolitan he came, donned his bear -- skin, which he fastened with a wire nail, and started the long climb. His sledge he carefully hid on the second floor, in an office at the left of the stairway.

"Don't think much of this hammer, after all," said he. "What I need is an ax. Perhaps this afternoon I can have another go at that hardware place and find one.

"If the handle's gone, I can heft it with green wood. With a good ax and these two revolvers -- till I find some rifles -- I guess we're safe enough, spearheads or not!"

About him he glanced at the ever-present molder and decay. This office, he could easily see, had been both spacious and luxurious, but now it offered a sorry spectacle. In the dust over by a window something glittered dully.

Stern found it was a fragment of a beveled mirror, which had probably hung there and, when the frame rotted, had dropped. He brushed it off and looked eagerly into it.

A cry of amazement burst from him.

"Do I look like that?" he shouted. "Well, I won't, for long!"

He propped the glass up on the steel beam of the window-opening, and got the scissors out of the bag. Ten minutes later, the face of Allan Stern bore some resemblance to its original self. True enough, his hair remained a bit jagged, especially in the back, his brows were somewhat uneven, and the point to which his beard was trimmed was far from perfect.

But none the less his wild savagery had given place to a certain aspect of civilization that made the white bearskin over his shoulders look doubly strange.

Stern, however, was well pleased. He smiled in satisfaction.

"What will she think, and say?" he wondered, as he once more took up the bag and started on the long, exhausting climb.

Sweating profusely, badly "blown," -- for he had not taken much time to rest on the way -- the engineer at last reached his offices in the tower.

Before entering, he called the girl's name.

"Beatrice! Oh, Beatrice! Are you awake, and visible?"

"All right, come in!" she answered cheerfully, and came to meet him in the doorway. Out to him she stretched her hand, in welcome; and the smile she gave him set his heart pounding.

He had to laugh at her astonishment and naive delight over his changed appearance; but all the time his eyes were eagerly devouring her beauty.

For now, freshly-awakened, full of new life and vigor after a sound night's sleep, the girl was magnificent.

The morning light disclosed new glints of color in her wondrous hair, as it lay broad and silken on the tiger-skin.

This she had secured at the throat and waist with bits of metal taken from the wreckage of the filing-cabinet.

Stern promised himself that ere long he would find her a profusion of gold pins and chains, in some of the Fifth Avenue shops, to serve her purposes till she could fashion real clothing.

As she gave him her hand, the Bengal skin fell back from her round, warm, cream-white arm.

At sight of it, at vision of that messy crown of hair and of those gray, penetrant, questioning eyes, the man's spent breath quickened.

He turned his own eyes quickly away, lest she should read his thought, and began speaking -- of what? He hardly knew. Anything, till he could master himself.

But through it all he knew that in his whole life, till now self-centered, analytical, cold, he never had felt such real, spontaneous happiness.

The touch of her fingers, soft and warm, dispelled his every anxiety. The thought that he was working, now, for her; serving her; striving to preserve and keep her, thrilled him with joy.

And as some foregleam of the future came to him, his fears dropped from him like those outworn rags he had discarded in the forest.

"Well, so we're both up and at it, again," he exclaimed, common-placely enough, his voice a bit uncertain. Stern had walked narrow girders six hundred feet sheer up; he had worked in caissons under tide-water, with the air-pumps driving full tilt to keep death out.

He had swung in a bosun's-chair down the face of the Yosemite Cañon at Cathedral Spires. But never had he felt emotions such as now. And greatly he marveled.

"I've had luck," he continued. "See here, and here?"

He showed her his treasures, all the contents of the bag, except the spear-point. Then, giving her the Cosmos bottle, he bade her drink. Gratefully she did so, while he explained to her the finding of the spring.

Her face aglow with eagerness and brave enthusiasm, she listened. But when he told her about the bathing-pool, an envious expression came to her.

"It's not fair," she protested, "for you to monopolize that. If you'll show me the place -- and just stay around in the woods, to see that nothing hurts me -- "

"You'll take a dip, too?"

Eagerly she nodded, her eyes beaming.

"I'm just dying for one!" she exclaimed. "Think! I haven't had a bath, now, for x years!"

"I'm at your service," declared the engineer. And for a moment a little silence came between them, a silence so profound that they could even hear the faint, far cheepings of the mud-swallows in the tower stair, above.

At the back of Stern's brain still lurked a haunting fear of the wood, of what the assegai-point might portend, but he dispelled it.

"Well, come along down," bade he. "It's getting late, already. But first, we must take just one more look, by this fresh morning light, from the platform up above, there?"

She assented readily. Together, talking of their first urgent needs, of their plans for this new day and for this wonderful, strange life that now confronted them, they climbed the stairs again. Once more they issued out on to the weed-grown platform of red tiles.

There they stood a moment, looking out with wonder over that vast, still, marvelous prospect of life-in-death. Suddenly the engineer spoke.

"Tell me," said he, "where did you get that line of verse you quoted last night? The one about this vast city -- heart all lying still, you know?"

"That? Why, that was from Wordsworth's Sonnet on London Bridge, of course," she smiled up at him. "You remember it now, don't you?"

"No-o," he disclaimed a trifle dubiously. "I -- that is, I never was much on poetry, you understand. It wasn't exactly in my line. But never mind. How did it go? I'd like to hear it, tremendously."

"I don't just recall the whole poem," she answered thoughtfully. "But I know part of it ran:

'...... This city now doth like a garment wear
The beauty of the morning. Silent, bare,
Ships, towers, domes, theaters, and temples lie
Open unto the fields and to the sky
All bright and glittering in the smokeless air.'"

A moment she paused to think. The sun, lancing its long and level rays across the water and the vast dead city, irradiated her face.

Instinctively, as she looked abroad over that wondrous panorama, she raised both bare arms; and, clad in the tiger-skin alone, stood for a little space like some Parsee priestess, sun-worshiping, on her tower of silence.

Stern looked at her, amazed.

Was this, could this indeed be the girl he had employed, in the old days -- the other days of routine and of tedium, of orders and specifications and dry-as-dust dictation? As though from a strange spell he aroused himself.

"The poem?" exclaimed he. "What next?"

"Oh, that? I'd almost forgotten about that; I was dreaming. It goes this way, I think:

'Never did the sun more beautifully steep
In his first splendor valley, rock, or hill,
Ne'er saw I, never felt a calm so deep;
The river glideth at his own sweet will.
Dear God! the very houses seem asleep,
And all this mighty heart is standing still!......'"

She finished the tremendous classic almost in a whisper.

They both stood silent a moment, gazing out together on that strange, inexplicable fulfilment of the poet's vision.

Up to them, through the crystal morning air, rose a faint, small sound of waters, from the brooklet in the forest. The nesting birds, below, were busy "in song and solace"; and through the golden sky above, a swallow slanted on sharp wing toward some unseen, leafy goal.

Far out upon the river, faint specks of white wheeled and hovered -- a flock of swooping gulls, snowy and beautiful and free. Their pinions flashed, spiralled and sank to rest on the wide waters.

Stern breathed a sigh. His right arm slipped about the sinuous, fur-robed body of the girl.

"Come, now!" said he, with returning practicality. "Bath for you, breakfast for both of us -- then we must buckle down to work. Come!"

10. Terror

Noon found them far advanced in the preliminaries of their hard adventuring.

Working together in a strong and frank companionship -- the past temporarily forgotten and the future still put far away -- half a day's labor advanced them a long distance on the road to safety.

Even these few hours sufficed to prove that, unless some strange, untoward accident befell, they stood a more than equal chance of winning out.

Realizing to begin with, that a home on the forty-eighth story of the tower was entirely impractical, since it would mean that most of their time would have to be used in laborious climbing, they quickly changed their dwelling.

They chose a suite of offices on the fifth floor, looking directly out over and into the cool green beauty of Madison Forest. In an hour or so, they cleared out the bats and spiders, the rubbish and the dust, and made the place very decently presentable.

"Well, that's a good beginning, anyhow," remarked the engineer, standing back and looking critically at the finished work.

"I don't see why we shouldn't make a fairly comfortable home out of this, for a while. It's not too high for ease, and it's high enough for safety -- to keep prowling bears and wolves and -- and other things from exploring us in the night."

He laughed, but memories of the spear-head tinged his merriment with apprehension. "In a day or two I'll make some kind of an outer door, or barricade. But first, I need that ax and some other things. Can you spare me for a while, now?"

"I'd rather go along, too," she answered wistfully, from the window-sill where she sat resting.

"No, not this time, please!" he entreated. "First I've got to go way to the top of the tower and bring down my chemicals and all the other things up there.

"Then I'm going out on a hunt for dishes, a lamp, some oil and no end of things. You save your strength for a while; stay here and keep house and be a good girl!"

"All right," she acceded, smiling a little sadly. "But really, I feel quite able to go."

"This afternoon, perhaps; not now. Goodby!" And he started for the door. Then a thought struck him. He turned and came back.

"By the way," said he, "if we can fix up some kind of a holster, I'll take one of those revolvers. With the best of this leather here," nodding at the Gladstone bag, "I should imagine we could manufacture something serviceable."

They planned the holster together, and he cut it out with his knife, while she slit leather thongs to lash it with. Presently it was done, and a strap to tie it round his waist with -- a crude, rough thing, but just as useful as though finished with the utmost skill.

"We'll make another for you when I get home this noon," he remarked picking up the automatic and a handful of cartridges. Quickly he filled the magazine. The shells were green with verdigris, and many a rust-spot disfigured the one-time brightness of the arm.

As he stepped over to the window, aimed and pulled the trigger, a sharp and welcome report burst from the weapon. And a few leaves, clipped from an oak in the forest, zigzagged down in the bright, warm sunlight.

"I guess she'll do all right!" he laughed, sliding the ugly weapon into his new holster. "You see, the powder and fulminate, sealed up in the cartridges, are practically imperishable. Here, let me load yours, too.

"If you want something to do, you can practice on that dead limb out there, see? And don't be afraid of wasting ammunition. There must be millions of cartridges in this old burg -- millions -- all ours!"

Again he laughed, and handing her the other pistol, now fully loaded, took his leave. Before he had climbed a hundred feet up the tower stair, he heard a slow, uneven pop -- pop -- popping, and with satisfaction knew that Beatrice was already perfecting herself in the use of the revolver.

"And she may need it, too -- we both may, badly -- before we know it!" thought he, frowning, as he kept upon his way.

This reflection weighed in so heavily upon him, all due to the flint assegai-point, that he made still another excuse that afternoon and so got out of taking the girl into the forest with him on his exploring trip.

The excuse was all the more plausible inasmuch as he left her enough work at home to do, making some real clothing and some sandals for them both. This task, now that the girl had scissors to use, was not too hard.

Stern brought her great armfuls of the furs from the shop in the arcade, and left her busily and happily employed.

He spent the afternoon in scouting through the entire neighborhood from Sixth Avenue as far east as Third and from Twenty-Seventh Street down through Union Square.

Revolver in his left hand, knife in his right to cut away troublesome bush or brambles, or to slit impeding vine-masses, he progressed slowly and observantly.

He kept his eyes open for big game, but -- though he found moose-tracks at the corner of Broadway and Nineteenth -- he ran into nothing more formidable than a lynx which snarled at him from a tree overhanging the mournful ruins of the Farragut monument.

One shot sent it bounding and screaming with pain, out of view. Stern noted with satisfaction that blood followed its trail.

"Guess I haven't forgotten how to shoot in all these x years!" he commented, stooping to examine the spoor. "That may come in handy later!"

Then, still wary and watchful, he continued his exploration.

He found that the city, as such, had entirely ceased to be.

"Nothing but lines and monstrous rubbish-heaps of ruins," he sized up the situation, "traversed by lanes of forest and overgrown with every sort of vegetation.

"Every wooden building completely wiped out. Brick and

stone ones practically gone. Steel alone standing, and that in rotten shape. Nothing at all intact but the few concrete structures.

"Ha! ha!" And he laughed satirically. "If the builders of the twentieth century could have foreseen this they wouldn't have thrown quite such a chest, eh? And they talked of engineering!"

Useless though it was, he felt a certain pride in noting that the Osterhaut Building, on Seventeenth Street, had lasted rather better than the average.

"My work!" said he, nodding with grim satisfaction, then passed on.

Into the Subway he penetrated at Eighteenth Street, climbing with difficulty down the choked stairway, through bushes and over masses of ruin that had fallen from the roof. The great tube, he saw, was choked with litter.

Slimy and damp it was, with a mephitic smell and ugly pools of water settled in the ancient road-bed. The rails were wholly gone in places. In others only rotten fragments of steel remained.

A goggle-eyed toad stared impudently at him from a long tangle of rubbish that had been a train -- stalled there forever by the final block-signal of death.

Through the broken arches overhead the rain and storms of ages had beaten down, and lush grasses flourished here and there, where sunlight could penetrate.

No human dust-heaps here, as in the shelter of the arcade. Long since every vestige of man had been swept away. Stern shuddered, more depressed by the sight here than at any other place so far visited.

"And they boasted of a work for all time!" whispered he, awed by the horror of it. "They boasted -- like the financiers, the churchmen, the merchants, everybody! Boasted of their institutions, their city, their country. And now -- "

Out he clambered presently, terribly depressed by what he had witnessed, and set to work laying in still more supplies from the wrecked shops. Now for the first time, his wonder and astonishment having largely abated, he began to feel the horror of this loneliness.

"No life here! Nobody to speak to -- except the girl..." he exclaimed aloud, the sound of his own voice uncanny in that woodland street of death. "All gone, everything! My Heavens, suppose I didn't have her? How long could I go on alone, and keep my mind?"

The thought terrified him. He put it resolutely away and went to work. Wherever he stumbled upon anything of value he eagerly seized it.

The labor, he found, kept him from the subconscious dread of what might happen to Beatrice or to himself if either should meet with any mishap. The consequences of either one dying, he knew, must be horrible beyond all thinking for the survivor.

Up Broadway he found much to keep -- things which he garnered in the up-caught hem of his bearskin, things of all kinds and uses. He found a clay pipe -- all the wooden ones had vanished from the shop -- and a glass jar of tobacco.

These he took as priceless treasures. More jars of edibles he discovered, also a stock of rare wines. Coffee and salt he came upon. In the ruins of the little French brass-ware shop, opposite the Flatiron, he made a rich haul of cups and plates and a still serviceable lamp.

Strangely enough, it still had oil in it. The fluid hermetically sealed in, had not been able to evaporate.

At last, when the lengthening shadows in Madison Forest warned him that day was ending, he betook himself, heavy laden, once more back past the spring, and so through the path which already was beginning to be visible back to the shelter of the Metropolitan.

"Now for a great surprise for the girl!" thought he, laboriously toiling up the stair with his burden: "What will she say, I wonder, when she sees all these housekeeping treasures?" Eagerly he hastened.

But before he had reached the third story he heard a cry from above. Then a spatter of revolver-shots punctured the air.

He stopped, listening in alarm.

"Beatrice! Oh, Beatrice!" he hailed, his voice falling flat and stifled in those ruinous passages.

Another shot.

"Answer!" panted Stern. "What's the matter now?"

Hastily he put down his burden, and, spurred by a great terror, bounded up the broken stairs.

Into their little shelter, their home, he ran, calling her name.

No reply came!

Stern stopped short, his face a livid gray.

"Merciful Heaven!" stammered he.

The girl was gone!

11. A Thousand Years!

Sickened with a numbing anguish of fear such as in all his life he had never known, Stern stood there a moment, motionless and lost.

Then he turned. Out into the hall he ran, and his voice, re-echoing wildly, rang through those long-deserted aisles.

All at once he heard a laugh behind him -- a hail.

He wheeled about, trembling and spent. Out his arms went, in eager greeting. For the girl, laughing and flushed, and very beautiful, was coming down the stair at the end of the hall.

Never had the engineer beheld a sight so wonderful to him as this woman, clad in the Bengal robe; this girl who smiled and ran to meet him.

"What? Were you frightened?" she asked, growing suddenly serious, as he stood there speechless and pale. "Why -- what could happen to me here?"

His only answer was to take her in his arms and whisper her name. But she struggled to be free.

"Don't! you mustn't!" she exclaimed. "I didn't mean to alarm you. Didn't even know you were here!"

"I heard the shots -- I called -- you didn't answer. Then -- "

"You found me gone? I didn't hear you. It was nothing, after all. Nothing -- much!"

He led her back into the room.

"What happened? Tell me!"

"It was really too absurd!"

"What was it?"

"Only this," and she laughed again. "I was getting supper ready, as you see," with a nod at their provision laid out upon the clean-brushed floor. "When -- "

"Yes?"

"Why, a blundering great hawk swooped in through the window there, circled around, pounced on the last of our beef and tried to fly away with it."

Stern heaved a sigh of relief. "So that was all?" asked he. "But the shots? And your absence?"

"I struck at him. He showed fight. I blocked the window. He was determined to get away with the food. I was determined he shouldn't. So I snatched the revolver and opened fire."

"And then?"

"That confused him. He flapped out into the hall. I chased him. Away up the stairs he circled. I shot again. Then I pursued. Went up two stories. But he must have got away through some opening or other. Our beef's all gone!" And Beatrice looked very sober.

"Never mind, I've got a lot more stuff downstairs. But tell me, did you wing him?"

"I'm afraid not," she admitted. "There's a feather or two on the stairs, though."

"Good work!" cried he laughing, his fear all swallowed in the joy of having found her again, safe and unhurt. "But please don't give me another such panic, will you? It's all right this time, however.

"And now if you'll just wait here and not get fighting with any more wild creatures, I'll go down and bring my latest finds. I like your pluck," he added slowly, gazing earnestly at her.

"But I don't want you chasing things in this old shell of a building. No telling what crevice you might fall into or what accident might happen. Au revoir!"

Her smile as he left her was inscrutable, but her eyes, strangely bright, followed him till he had vanished once more down the stairs.

★ ★ ★ ★ ★

Broad strokes, a line here, one there, with much left to the imagining -- such will serve best for the painting of a picture like this -- a picture wherein every ordinary bond of human life, the nexus of man's society, is shattered. Where everything must strive to reconstruct itself from the dust. Where the future, if any such there may be, must rise from the ashes of a crumbling past.

Broad strokes, for detailed ones would fill too vast a canvas. Impossible to describe a tenth of the activities of Beatrice and Stern the next four days. Even to make a list of their hard-won possessions would turn this chapter into a mere catalogue.

So let these pass for the most part. Day by day the man, issuing forth sometimes alone, sometimes with Beatrice, labored like a Titan among the ruins of New York.

Though more than ninety per cent. of the city's one-time wealth had long since vanished, and though all standards of worth had wholly changed, yet much remained to harvest.

Infinitudes of things, more or less damaged, they bore up to their shelter, up the stairs which here and there Stern had repaired with rough-hewn logs.

For now he had an ax, found in that treasure-house of Currier & Brown's, brought to a sharp edge on a wet, flat stone by the spring, and hefted with a sapling.

This implement was of incredible use, and greatly enheartened the engineer. More valuable it was than a thousand tons of solid gold.

The same store yielded also a well-preserved enameled water-pail and some smaller dishes of like ware, three more knives, quantities of nails, and some small tools; also the tremendous bonanza of a magazine rifle and a shotgun, both of which Stern judged would come into shape by the application of oil and by careful tinkering. Of ammunition, here and elsewhere, the engineer had no doubt he could unearth unlimited quantities.

"With steel," he reflected, "and with my flint spearhead, I can make fire at any time. Wood is plenty, and there's lots of 'punk.' So the first step in reestablishing civilization is secure. With fire, everything else becomes possible.

"After a while, perhaps, I can get around to manufacturing matches again. But for the present my few ounces of phosphorus and the flint and steel will answer very well."

Beatrice, like the true woman she was, addressed herself eagerly to the fascinating task of making a real home out of the barren desolation of the fifth floor offices. Her splendid energy was no less than the engineer's. And very soon a comfortable air pervaded the place.

Stern manufactured a broom for her by cutting willow withes and lashing them with hide strips onto a trimmed branch. Spiders and dust all vanished. A true housekeeping appearance set in.

To supplement the supply of canned food that accumulated along one of the walls, Stern shot what game he could -- squirrels, partridges and rabbits.

Metal dishes, especially of solid gold, ravished from Fifth Avenue shops, took their place on the crude table he had fashioned with his ax. Not for esthetic effect did they now value gold, but merely because that metal had perfectly withstood the ravages of time.

In the ruins of a magnificent store near Thirty-First Street, Stern found a vault burst open by frost and slow disintegration of the steel.

Here something over a quart of loose diamonds, big and little, rough and cut, were lying in confusion all about. Stern took none of these. Their value now was no greater than that of any pebble.

But he chose a massive clasp of gold for Beatrice, for that could serve to fasten her robe. And in addition he gathered up a few rings and onetime costly jewels which could be worn. For the girl, after all, was one of Eve's daughters.

Bit by bit he accumulated many necessary articles, including some tooth-brushes which he found sealed in glass bottles, and a variety of gold toilet articles. Use was his first consideration now. Beauty came far behind.

In the corner of their rooms, after a time, stood a fair variety of tools, some already serviceable, others waiting to be polished, ground and hefted, and in some cases retempered. Two rough chairs made their appearance.

The north room, used only for cooking, became their forge and oven all in one. For here, close to a window where the smoke could drift out, Stern built a circular stone fireplace.

And here Beatrice presided over her copper casseroles and saucepans from the little shop on Broadway. Here, too, Stern planned to construct a pair of skin bellows, and presently to set up the altars of Vulcan and of Tubal Cain once more.

Both of them "thanked whatever gods there be" that the girl was a good cook. She amazed the engineer by the variety of dishes she managed to concoct from the canned goods, the game that Stern shot, and fresh dandelion greens dug near the spring. These edibles, with the blackest of black coffee, soon had them in fine fettle.

"I certainly have begun to put on weight," laughed the man after dinner on the fourth day, as he lighted his fragrant pipe with a roll of blazing birch-bark.

"My bearskin is getting tight. You'll have to let it out for me, or else stop such magic in the kitchen."

She smiled back at him, sitting there at ease in the sunshine by the window, sipping her coffee out of a gold cup with a solid gold spoon.

Stern, feeling the May breeze upon his face, hearing the bird-songs in the forest depths, felt a wellbeing, a glow of health and joy such as he had never in his whole life known -- the health of outdoor labor and sound sleep and perfect digestion, the joy of accomplishment and of the girl's near presence.

"I suppose we do live pretty well," she answered, surveying the remnants of the feast. "Potted tongue and peas, fried squirrel, partridge and coffee ought to satisfy anybody. But still -- "

"What is it?"

"I would like some buttered toast and some cream for my coffee, and some sugar."

Stern laughed heartily.

"You don't want much!" he exclaimed, vastly amused, the while he blew a cloud of Latakia smoke. "Well, you be patient, and everything will come, in time.

"You mustn't expect me to do magic. On the fourth day you don't imagine I've had time enough to round up the ten thousandth descendant of the erstwhile cow, do you?

"Or grow cane and make sugar? Or find grain for seed, clear some land, plow, harrow, plant, hoe, reap, winnow, grind and bolt and present you with a bag of prime flour? Now really?"

She pouted at his raillery. For a moment there was silence, while he drew at his pipe. At the girl he looked a little while. Then, his eyes a bit far-away, he remarked in a tone he tried to render casual:

"By the way, Beatrice, it occurs to me that we're doing rather well for old people -- very old."

She looked up with a startled glance.

"Very?" she exclaimed. "You know how old then?"

"Very, indeed!" he answered. "Yes, I've got some sort of an idea about it. I hope it won't alarm you when you know."

"Why -- how so? Alarm me?" she queried with a strange expression.

"Yes, because, you see, it's rather a long time since we went to sleep. Quite so. You see, I've been doing a little calculating, off and on, at odd times. Been putting two and two together, as it were.

"First, there was the matter of the dust in sheltered places, to guide me. The rate of deposition of what, in one or two spots, can't have been anything less than cosmic or star-dust, is fairly certain.

"Then again, the rate of this present deterioration of stone and steel has furnished another index. And last night I had a little peek at the pole-star, through my telescope, while you were asleep.

"The good old star has certainly shifted out of place a bit. Furthermore, I've been observing certain evolutionary changes in the animals and plants about us. Those have helped, too."

"And -- and what have you found out?" asked she with tremulous interest.

"Well, I think I've got the answer, more or less correctly. Of course it's only an approximate result, as we say in engineering. But the different items check up with some degree of consistency.

"And I'm safe in believing I'm within at least a hundred years of the date one way or the other. Not a bad factor of safety, that, with my limited means of working."

The girl's eyes widened. From her hand fell the empty gold cup; it rolled away across the clean-swept floor.

"What?" cried she. "You've got it, within a hundred years! Why, then -- you mean it's more than a hundred?"

Indulgently the engineer smiled.

"Come, now," he coaxed. "Just guess, for instance, how old you really are -- and growing younger every day?"

"Two hundred maybe? Oh surely not as old as that! It's horrible to think of!"

"Listen," bade he. "If I count your twenty-four years, when you went to sleep, you're now -- "

"What?"

"You're now at the very minimum calculation, just about one thousand and twenty-four! Some age, that, eh?"

Then, as she stared at him wide-eyed he added with a smile.

"No disputing that fact, no dodging it. The thing's as certain as that you're now the most beautiful woman in the whole wide world!"

12. Drawing Together

Days passed, busy days, full of hard labor and achievement, rich in experience and learning, in happiness, in dreams of what the future might yet bring.

Beatrice made and finished a considerable wardrobe of garments for them both. These, when the fur had been clipped close with the scissors, were not oppressively warm, and, even though on some days a bit uncomfortable, the man and woman tolerated them because they had no others.

Plenty of bathing and good food put them in splendid physical condition, to which their active exercise contributed much. And thus, judging partly by the state of the foliage, partly by the height of the sun, which Stern determined with considerable accuracy by means of a simple, home-made quadrant -- they knew mid-May was past and June was drawing near.

The housekeeping by no means took up all the girl's time. Often she went out with him on what he called his "pirating expeditions," that now sometimes led them as far afield as the sad ruins of the wharves and piers, or to the stark desolation and wreckage of lower Broadway and the onetime busy hives of newspaperdom, or up to Central Park or to the great remains of the two railroad terminals.

These two places, the former tide-gates of the city's life, impressed Stern most painfully of anything. The disintegrated tracks, the jumbled remains of locomotives and luxurious Pullmans with weeds growing rank upon them, the sunlight beating down through the caved-in roof of the Pennsylvania station concourse, where millions of human beings once had trod in all the haste of men's paltry, futile affairs, filled him with melancholy, and he was glad to get away again leaving the place to the jungle, the birds and beasts that now laid claim to it.

"*Sic transit gloria mundi!*" he murmured, as with sad eyes he mused upon the down-tumbled columns along the facade, the overgrown entrance-way, the cracked and falling arches and architraves. "And this, they said, was builded for all time!"

It was on one of these expeditions that the engineer found and pocketed -- unknown to Beatrice -- another disconcerting relic.

This was a bone, broken and splintered, and of no very great age, gnawed with perfectly visible tooth-marks. He picked it up, by chance, near the west side of the ruins of the old City Hall.

Stern recognized the manner in which the bone had been cracked open with a stone to let the marrow be sucked out. The sight of this gruesome relic revived all his fears, tenfold more acutely than ever, and filled him with a sense of vague, impending evil, of peril deadly to them both.

This was the more keen, because the engineer knew at a glance that the bone was the upper end of a human femur -- human, or, at the very least, belonging to some highly anthropoid animal. And of apes or gorillas he had, as yet, found no trace in the forests of Manhattan.

Long he mused over his find. But not a single word did he ever say to Beatrice concerning it or the flint spear-point. Only he kept his eyes and ears well open for other bits of corroborative evidence.

And he never ventured a foot from the building unless his rifle and revolver were with him, their magazines full of high-power shells.

The girl always went armed, too, and soon grew to be such an expert shot that she could drop a squirrel from the tip of a fir, or wing a heron in full flight.

Once her quick eyes spied a deer in the tangles of the one-time Gramercy Park, now no longer neatly hedged with iron palings, but spread in wild confusion that joined the riot of growth beyond.

On the instant she fired, wounding the creature.

Stern's shot, echoing hers, missed. Already the deer was away, out of range through the forest. With some difficulty they pursued down a glen-like strip of woods that must have once been Irving Place.

Two hundred yards south of the park they sighted the animal again. And the girl with a single shot sent it crashing to earth.

"Bravo, Diana!" hurrahed Stern, running forward with enthusiasm. The "deer fever" was on him, as strong as in his old days in the Hudson Bay country. Hot was the pleasure of the kill when that meant food. As he ran he jerked his knife from the skin sheath the girl had made for him.

Thus they had fresh venison to their heart's content -- venison broiled over white-hot coals in the fireplace, juicy and savory -- sweet beyond all telling.

A good deal of the meat they smoked and salted down for future use. Stern undertook to tan the hide with strips of hemlock bark laid in a water pit dug near the spring. He added also some oak-bark, nut-galls and a good quantity of young sumac shoots.

"I guess that ought to hit the mark if anything will," remarked he, as he immersed the skin and weighed it down with rocks.

"It's like the old 'shotgun' prescriptions of our extinct doctors -- a little of everything, bound to do the trick, one way or another."

The great variety of labors now imposed upon him began to try his ingenuity to the full. In spite of all his wealth of practical knowledge and his scientific skill, he was astounded at the huge demands of even the simplest human life.

The girl and he now faced these, without the social cooperation which they had formerly taken entirely for granted, and the change of conditions had begun to alter Stern's concepts of almost everything.

He was already beginning to realize how true the old saying was: "One man is no man!" and how the world had been the world merely because of the interrelations, the interdependencies of human beings in vast numbers.

He was commencing to get a glimpse of the vanished social

problems that had enmeshed civilization, in their true light, now that all he confronted and had to struggle with was the unintelligent and overbearing dominance of nature.

All this was of huge value to the engineer. And the strong individualism (essentially anarchistic) on which he had prided himself a thousand years ago, was now beginning to receive some mortal blows, even during these first days of the new, solitary, unsocialized life.

But neither he nor the girl had very much time for introspective thought. Each moment brought its immediate task, and every day seemed busier than the last had been.

At meals, however, or at evening, as they sat together by the light of their lamp in the now homelike offices, Stern and Beatrice found pleasure in a little random speculation. Often they discussed the catastrophe and their own escape.

Stern brought to mind some of Professor Raoul Pictet's experiments with animals, in which the Frenchman had suspended animation for long periods by sudden freezing. This method seemed to answer, in a way, the girl's earlier questions as to how they had escaped death in the many long winters since they had gone to sleep.

Again, they tried to imagine the scenes just following the catastrophe, the horror of that long-past day, and the slow, irrevocable decay of all the monuments of the human race.

Often they talked till past midnight, by the glow of their stone fireplace, and many were the aspects of the case that they developed. These hours seemed to Stern the happiest of his life.

For the rapprochement between this beautiful woman and himself at such times became very close and fascinatingly intimate, and Stern felt, little by little, that the love which now was growing deep within his heart for her was not without its answer in her own.

But for the present the man restrained himself and spoke no overt word. For that, he understood, would immediately have put all things on a different basis -- and there was urgent work still waiting to be done.

"There's no doubt in my mind," said he one day as they sat

talking, "that you and I are absolutely the last human beings -- civilized I mean -- left alive anywhere in the world.

"If anybody else had been spared, whether in Chicago or San Francisco, in London, Paris or Hong-Kong, they'd have made some determined effort before now to get in touch with New York. This, the prime center of the financial and industrial world, would have been their first objective point."

"But suppose," asked she, "there were others, just a few here or there, and they'd only recently waked up, like ourselves. Could they have succeeded in making themselves known to us so soon?"

He shook a dubious head.

"There may be some one else, somewhere," he answered slowly, "but there's nobody else in this part of the world, anyhow. Nobody in this particular Eden but just you and me. To all intents and purposes I'm Adam. And you -- well, you're Eve! But the tree? We haven't found that -- yet."

She gave him a quick, startled glance, then let her head fall, so that he could not see her eyes. But up over her neck, her cheek and even to her temples, where the lustrous masses of hair fell away, he saw a tide of color mount.

And for a little space the man forgot to smoke. At her he gazed, a strange gleam in his eyes.

And no word passed between them for a while. But their thoughts -- ?

13. The Great Experiment

The idea that there might possibly be others of their kind in far-distant parts of the earth worked strongly on the mind of the girl. Next day she broached the subject again to her companion.

"Suppose," theorized she, "there might be a few score of others, maybe a few hundred, scattered here and there? They might awaken one by one, only to die, if less favorably situated than we happen to be. Perhaps thousands may have slept, like us, only to wake up to starvation!"

"There's no telling, of course," he answered seriously. "Undoubtedly that may be very possible. Some may have escaped the great death, on high altitudes -- on the Eiffel Tower, for instance, or on certain mountains or lofty plateaus. The most we can do for the moment is just to guess at the probabilities. And -- "

"But if there are people elsewhere?" she interrupted eagerly, her eyes glowing with hope, "isn't there any way to get in touch with them? Why don't we hunt? Suppose only one or two in each country should have survived; if we could get them all together again in a single colony -- don't you see?"

"You mean the different languages and arts and all the rest might still be preserved? The colony might grow and flourish, and mankind again take possession of the earth and conquer it, in a few decades? Yes, of course. But even though there shouldn't be anybody else, there's no cause for despair. Of that, however, we won't speak now."

"But why don't we try to find out about it?" she persisted. "If there were only the remotest chance -- "

"By Jove, I will try it!" exclaimed the engineer, fired with a new thought, a fresh ambition. "How? I don't know just yet, but I'll see. There'll be a way, right enough, if I can only think it out!"

That afternoon he made his way down Broadway, past the copper-shop, to the remains of the telegraph office opposite the Flatiron.

Into it he penetrated with some difficulty. A mournful sight it was, this one-time busy ganglion of the nation's nerve-system. Benches and counters were quite gone, instruments corroded past recognition, everything in hideous disorder.

But in a rear room Stern found a large quantity of copper wire. The wooden drums on which it had been wound were gone; the insulation had vanished, but the coils of wire still remained.

"Fine!" said the explorer, gathering together several coils. "Now when I get this over to the Metropolitan, I think the first step toward success will have been taken."

By nightfall he had accumulated enough wire for his tentative experiments. Next day he and the girl explored the remains of the old wireless station on the roof of the building, overlooking Madison Avenue.

They reached the roof by climbing out of a window on the east side of the tower and descending a fifteen-foot ladder that Stern had built for the purpose out of rough branches.

"You see it's fairly intact as yet," remarked the engineer, gesturing at the bread expanse. "Only, falling stones have made holes here and there. See how they yawn down into the rooms below! Well, come on, follow me. I'll tap with the ax, and if the roof holds me you'll be safe."

Thus, after a little while, they found a secure path to the little station.

This diminutive building, fortunately constructed of concrete, still stood almost unharmed. Into it they penetrated through the crumbling door. The winds of heaven had centuries ago swept away all trace of the ashes of the operator.

But there still stood the apparatus, rusted and sagging and dis-ordered, yet to Stern's practiced eye showing signs of promise. An hour's careful overhauling convinced the engineer that something might yet be accomplished.

And thus they set to work in earnest.

First, with the girl's help, he strung his copper-wire antennae from the tiled platform of the tower to the roof of the wireless station. Rough work this was, but answering the purpose as well as though of the utmost finish.

He connected up the repaired apparatus with these antennae, and made sure all was well. Then he dropped the wires over the side of the building to connect with one of the dynamos in the sub-basement.

All this took two and a half days of severe labor, in intervals of food-getting, cooking and household tasks. At last, when it was done --

"Now for some power!" exclaimed the engineer. And with his lamp he went down to inspect the dynamos again and to assure himself that his belief was correct, his faith that one or two of them could be put into running order.

Three of the machines gave little promise, for water had dripped in on them and they were rusted beyond any apparent rehabilitation. The fourth, standing nearest Twenty-Third Street, had by some freak of chance been protected by a canvas cover.

This cover was now only a mass of rotten rags, but it had at least safeguarded the machine for so long that no very serious deterioration had set in.

Stern worked the better part of a week with such tools as he could find or make -- he had to forge a wrench for the largest nuts -- "taking down" the dynamo, oiling, filing, polishing and repairing it, part by part.

The commutator was in bad shape and the brushes terribly corroded. But he tinkered and patched, hammered and heated and filed away, and at last putting the machine together again with terrible exertion, decided that it would run.

"Steam now!" was his next watchword, when he had wired the dynamo to connect with the station on the roof. And this was on the eighth day since he had begun his labor.

An examination of the boiler-room, which he reached by moving a ton of fallen stone-work from the doorway into the dynamo-room, encouraged him still further. As he penetrated into this place, feeble-shining lamp held on high, eyes eager to behold the prospect, he knew that success was not far away.

Down in these depths, almost as in the interior of the great Pyramid of Gizeh -- though the place smelled dank and close and stifling -- time seemed to have lost much of its destructive power. He chose one boiler that looked sound, and began looking for coal.

Of this he found a plentiful supply, well-preserved, in the bunkers. All one afternoon he labored, wheeling it in a steel barrow and dumping it in front of the furnace.

Where the smoke-stack led to and what condition it was in he knew not. He could not tell where the gases of combustion would escape to; but this he decided to leave to chance.

He grimaced at sight of the rusted flues and the steam-pipes connecting with the dynamo-room-pipes now denuded of their asbestos packing and leaky at several joints.

A strange, gnome-like picture he presented as he poked and pried in those dim regions, by the dim rays of the lamp. Spiders, roaches and a great gray rat or two were his only companions -- those, and hope.

"I don't know but I'm a fool to try and carry this thing out," said he, dubiously surveying the pipe. "I'm liable to start something here that I can't stop. Water-glasses leaky, gauges plugged up, safety-valve rusted into its seat -- the devil!"

But still he kept on. Something drove him inexorably forward. For he was an engineer -- and an American.

His next task was to fill the boiler. This he had to do by bringing water, two pails at a time from the spring. It took him three days.

Thus, after eleven days of heart-breaking lonely toil in that grimy dungeon, hampered for lack of tools, working with rotten materials, naked and sweaty, grimed, spent, profane, exhausted, everything was ready for the experiment -- the strangest, surely, in the annals of the human race.

He lighted up the furnace with dry wood, then stoked it full of coal. After an hour and a half his heart thrilled with mingled fear and exultation at sight of the steam, first white, then blue and thin, that began to hiss from the leaks in the long pipe.

"No way to estimate pressure, or anything," remarked he. "It's bull luck whether I go to hell or not!" And he stood back from the blinding glare of the furnace. With his naked arm he wiped the sweat from his streaming forehead.

"Bull luck!" repeated he. "But by the Almighty, I'll send that Morse, or bust!"

14. The Moving Lights

Panting with exhaustion and excitement, Stern made his way back to the engine-room. It was a strangely critical moment when he seized the corroded throttle-wheel to start the dynamo. The wheel stuck, and would not budge.

Stern, with a curse of sheer exasperation, snatched up his long spanner, shoved it through the spokes, and wrenched.

Groaning, the wheel gave way. It turned. The engineer hauled again.

"Go on!" shouted the man. "Start! Move!"

With a hissing plaint, as though rebellious against this awakening after its age-long sleep, the engine creaked into motion.

In spite of all Stern's oiling, every joint and bearing squealed in anguish. A rickety tremble possessed the engine as it gained speed. The dynamo began to hum with wild, strange protests of racked metal. The ancient "drive" of tarred hemp strained and quivered, but held.

And like the one-hoss shay about to collapse, the whole fabric of the resuscitated plant, leaking at a score of joints, creaking, whistling, shaking, voicing a hundred agonized mechanic woes, revived in a grotesque, absurd and shocking imitation of its onetime beauty and power.

At sight of this ghastly resurrection, the engineer (whose whole life had been passed in the love and service of machinery) felt a strange and sad emotion.

He sat down, exhausted, on the floor. In his hand the lamp trembled. Yet, all covered with sweat and dirt and rust as he was, this moment of triumph was one of the sweetest he had ever known.

He realized that this was now no time for inaction. Much yet remained to be done. So up he got again, and set to work.

First he made sure the dynamo was running with no serious defect and that his wiring had been made properly. Then he heaped the furnace full of coal, and closed the door, leaving only enough draft to insure a fairly steady heat for an hour or so.

This done, he toiled back up to where Beatrice was eagerly awaiting him in the little wireless station on the roof.

In he staggered, all but spent. Panting for breath, wild-eyed, his coal-blackened arms stretching out from the whiteness of the bear-skin, he made a singular picture.

"It's going!" he exclaimed. "I've got current -- it's good for a while, anyhow. Now -- now for the test!"

For a moment he leaned heavily against the concrete bench to which the apparatus was clamped. Already the day had drawn close to its end. The glow of evening had begun to fade a trifle, along the distant skyline; and beyond the Palisades a dull purple pall was settling down.

By the dim light that filtered through the doorway, Beatrice looked at his deep-lined, bearded face, now reeking with sweat and grimed with dust and coal. An ugly face -- but not to her. For through that mask she read the dominance, the driving force, the courage of this versatile, unconquerable man.

"Well," suddenly laughed Stern, with a strange accent in his voice, "well then, here goes for the operator in the Eiffel Tower, eh?"

Again he glanced keenly, in the failing light, at the apparatus there before him.

"She'll do, I guess," judged he, slipping on the rusted head-receiver. He laid his hand upon the key and tried a few tentative dots and dashes.

Breathless, the girl watched, daring no longer to question him. In the dielectric, the green sparks and spurts of living flame began to crackle and to hiss like living spirits of an unknown power.

Stern, feeling again harnessed to his touch the life-force of the world that once had been, exulted with a wild emotion. Yet, science-worshiper that he was, something of reverent awe tinged the keen triumph. A strange gleam dwelt within his eyes; and through his lips the breath came quick as he flung his very being into this supreme experiment.

He reached for the ondometer. Carefully, slowly, he "tuned up" the wave-lengths; up, up to five thousand metres, then back again; he ran the whole gamut of the wireless scale.

Out, ever out into the thickening gloom, across the void and vacancy of the dead world, he flung his lightnings in a wild appeal. His face grew hard and eager.

"Anything? Any answer?" asked Beatrice, laying a hand upon his shoulder -- a hand that trembled.

He shook his head in negation. Again he switched the roaring current on; again he hurled out into ether his cry of warning and distress, of hope, of invitation -- the last lone call of man to man -- of the last New Yorker to any other human being who, by the merest chance, might possibly hear him in the wreck of other cities, other lands. "S. O. S.!" crackled the green flame. "S.O.S.! S.O.S.! -- "

Thus came night, fully, as they waited, as they called and listened; as, together there in that tiny structure on the roof of the tremendous ruin, they swept the heavens and the earth with their wild call -- in vain.

Half an hour passed and still the engineer, grim as death, whirled the chained lightnings out and away.

"Nothing yet?" cried Beatrice at last, unable to keep silence any longer. "Are you quite sure you can't -- "

The question was not finished.

For suddenly, far down below them, as though buried in the entrails of the earth, shuddered a stifled, booming roar.

Through every rotten beam and fiber the vast wreck of the building vibrated. Some wall or other, somewhere, crumbled and went crashing down with a long, deep droning thunder that ended in a sliding diminuendo of noise.

"The boiler!" shouted Stern.

Off he flung the head-piece. He leaped up; he seized the girl.

Out of the place he dragged her. She screamed as a huge

weight from high aloft on the tower smashed bellowing through the roof, and with a shower of stones ripped its way down through the rubbish of the floors below, as easily as a bullet would pierce a newspaper.

The crash sent them recoiling. The whole roof shook and trembled like honey-combed ice in a spring thaw.

Down below, something rumbled, jarred, and came to rest.

Both of them expected nothing but that the entire structure would collapse like a card-house and shatter down in ruins that would be their death.

But though it swayed and quivered, as in the grasp of an earthquake, it held.

Stern circled Beatrice with his arm.

"Courage, now! Steady now, steady!" cried he.

The grinding, the booming of down-hurled stones and walls died away; the echoes ceased. A wind-whipped cloud of steam and smoke burst up, fanlike, beyond the edge of the roof. It bellied away, dim in the night, upon the stiff northerly breeze.

"Fire?" ventured the girl.

"No! Nothing to burn. But come, come; let's get out o' this anyhow. There's nothing doing, any more. All through! Too much risk staying up here, now."

Silent and dejected, they made their cautious way over the shaken roof. They walked with the greatest circumspection, to avoid falling through some new hole or freshly opened crevasse.

To Stern, especially, this accident was bitter. After nearly a fortnight's exhausting toil, the miserable fiasco was maddening.

"Look!" suddenly exclaimed the engineer, pointing. A vast, gaping cañon of blackness opened at their very feet -- a yawning gash forty feet long and ten or twelve broad, with roughly jagged edges, leading down into unfathomed depths below.

Stern gazed at it, puzzled, a moment, then peered up into the darkness above.

"H-m!" said he. "One of the half-ton hands of the big clock up there has just taken a drop, that's all. One drop too much, I call it. Now if we -- or our rooms -- had just happened to be underneath? Some excitement, eh?"

They circled the opening and approached the tower wall. Stern picked up the rough ladder, which had been shaken down from its place, and once more set it to the window through which they were to enter.

But even as Beatrice put her foot on the first rung, she started with a cry. Stern felt the grip of her trembling hand on his arm.

"What is it?" exclaimed he.

"Look! Look!"

Immobile with astonishment and fear, she stood pointing out and away, to westward, toward the Hudson.

Stern's eyes followed her hand.

He tried to cry out, but only stammered some broken, unintelligible thing.

There, very far away and very small, yet clearly visible in swarms upon the inky-black expanse of waters, a hundred, a thousand little points of light were moving.

15. Portents of War

Stern and Beatrice stood there a few seconds at the foot of the ladder, speechless, utterly at a loss for any words to voice the turmoil of confused thoughts awakened by this inexplicable apparition.

But all at once the girl, with a wordless cry, sank on her knees beside the vast looming bulk of the tower. She covered her face with both hands, and through her fingers the tears of joy began to flow.

"Saved -- oh, we're saved!" cried she. "There are people -- and they're coming for us!"

Stern glanced down at her, an inscrutable expression on his face, which had grown hard and set and ugly. His lips moved, as though he were saying something to himself; but no sound escaped them.

Then, quite suddenly, he laughed a mirthless laugh. To him vividly flashed back the memory of the flint spear-head and the gnawed leg-bone, cracked open so the marrow could be sucked out, all gashed with savage tooth-marks.

A certain creepy sensation began to develop along his spine. He felt a prickling on the nape of his neck, as the hair stirred there. Instinctively he reached for his revolver.

"So, then," he sneered at himself, "we're up against it, after all? And all my calculations about the world being swept clear, were so much punk? Well, well, this is interesting! Oh, I see it coming, all right -- good and plenty -- and soon!"

But the girl interrupted his ugly thoughts as he stood there straining his eyes out into the dark.

"How splendid! How glorious!" cried she. "Only to think that we're going to see people again! Can you imagine it?"

"Hardly."

"Why, what's the matter? You -- speak as though you weren't -- saved!"

"I didn't mean to. It's -- just surprise, I guess."

"Come! Let's signal them with a fire from the tower top. I'll help carry wood. Let's hurry down and run and meet them!"

Highly excited, the girl had got to her feet again, and now clutched the engineer's arm in burning eagerness.

"Let's go! Go -- at once! This minute!"

But he restrained her.

"You don't really think that would be quite prudent, do you?" asked he. "Not just yet?"

"Why not?"

"Why, can't you see? We -- that is, there is no way to tell -- "

"But they're coming to save us, can't you see? Somehow, somewhere, they must have caught that signal! And shall we wait, and perhaps let them lose us, after all?"

"Certainly not. But first we -- why, we ought to make quite sure, you understand. Sure that they -- they're really civilized, you know."

"But they must be, to have read the wireless!"

"Oh, you're counting on that, are you? Well, that's a big assumption. It won't do. No, we've got to go slow in this game. Got to wait. Wait, and see. Easy does it!"

He tried to speak boldly and with nonchalance, but the girl's keen ear detected at least a little of the emotion that was troubling him. She kept a moment's silence, while the quivering lights drew on and on, steadily, slowly, like a host of fireflies on the bosom of the night.

"Why don't you get the telescope, and see?" she asked, at length.

"No use. It isn't a night-glass. Couldn't see a thing."

"But anyhow, those lights mean men, don't they?"

"Naturally. But until we know what kind, we're better off right where we are. I'm willing to welcome the coming guest, all right, if he's peaceful. Otherwise, it's powder and ball, hot water, stones and things for him!"

The girl stared a moment at the engineer, while this new idea took root within her brain.

"You -- you don't mean," she faltered at last, "that these may be -- savages!"

He started at the word. "What makes you think that?" he parried, striving to spare her all needless alarm.

She pondered a moment, while the fire-dots, like a shoal of swimming stars, drew slowly nearer, nearer the Manhattan shore.

"Tell me, are they savages?"

"How do I know?"

"It's easy enough to see you've got an opinion about it. You think they're savages, don't you?"

"I think it's very possible."

"And if so -- what then?"

"What then? Why, in case they aren't mighty nice and kind, there'll be a hot time in the old town, that's all. And somebody'll get hurt. It won't be us!"

Beatrice asked no more, for a minute or two, but the engineer felt her fingers tighten on his arm.

"I'm with you, till the end!" she whispered.

Another pregnant silence, while the nightwind stirred her hair and wafted the warm feminine perfume of her to his nostrils. Stern took a long, deep breath. A sort of dizziness crept over him, as from a glass of wine on an empty stomach. The Call of Woman strove to master him, but he repelled it. And, watching the creeping lights, he spoke; spoke to himself as much as to the girl; spoke, lest he think too much.

"There's a chance, a mere possibility," said he, "that those boats, canoes, coracles or whatever they may be, belong to white people, far descendants of the few survivors of the cataclysm. There's some slight chance that these people may be civilized, or partly so.

"Why they're coming across the Hudson, at this time o' night, with what object and to what place, we can't even guess. All we can do is wait, and watch and -- be ready for anything."

"For anything!" she echoed. "You've seen me shoot! You know!"

He took her hand, and pressed it. And silence fell again, as the long vigil started, there in the shadow of the tower, on the roof.

For some quarter of an hour, neither spoke. Then at last, said Stern:

"See, now! The lights seem to be winking out. The canoes must have come close in toward the shore of the island. They're being masked behind the trees. The people -- whoever they are -- will be landing directly now!"

"And then?"

"Wait and see!"

They resigned themselves to patience. The girl's breath came quickly, as she watched. Even the engineer felt his heart throb with accelerated haste.

Now, far in the east, dim over the flat and dreary ruins of Long Island, the sky began to silver, through a thin veil of cirrus cloud. A pallid moon was rising. Far below, a breeze stirred the tree-fronds in Madison Forest. A bat staggered drunkenly about the tower, then reeled away into the gloom; and, high aloft, an owl uttered its melancholy plaint.

Beatrice shuddered.

"They'll be here pretty soon!" whispered she. "Hadn't we better go down, and get our guns? In case -- "

"Time enough," he answered. "Wait a while."

"Hark! What's that?" she exclaimed suddenly, holding her breath.

Off to northward, dull, muffled, all but inaudible, they both heard a rhythmic pulsing, strangely barbaric.

"Heavens!" ejaculated Stern. "War-drums! Tom-toms, as I live!"

16. The Gathering of the Hordes

"Tom-toms? So they are savages?" exclaimed the girl, taking a quick breath. "But -- what then?"

"Don't just know, yet. It's a fact, though; they're certainly savages. Two tribes, one with torches, one with drums. Two different kinds, I guess. And they're coming in here to parley or fight or something. Regular powwow on hand. Trouble ahead, whichever side wins!"

"For us?"

"That depends. Maybe we'll be able to lie hidden, here, till this thing blows over, whatever it may be. If not, and if they cut off our water-supply, well -- "

He ended with a kind of growl. The sound gave Beatrice a strange sensation. She kept a moment's silence, then remarked:

"They're up around Central Park now, the drums are, don't you think so? How far do you make that?"

"Close on to two miles. Come, let's be moving."

In silence they climbed the shaky ladder, reached the tower stairs and descended the many stories to their dwelling.

Here, the first thing Stern did was to strike a light, which he masked in a corner, behind a skin stretched like a screen from one wall to the other. By this illumination, very dim yet adequate, he minutely examined all their firearms.

He loaded every one to capacity and made sure all were in working order. Then he satisfied himself that the supply of cartridges was ample. These he laid carefully along by the windows overlooking Madison Forest, by the door leading into the suite of offices, and by the stair-head that gave access to the fifth floor.

Then he blew out the light again.

"Two revolvers, one shotgun, and one rifle, all told," said he.

"All magazine arms. I guess that'll hold them for a while, if it comes down to brass tacks! How's your nerve, Beatrice?"

"Never better!" she whispered, from the dark. He saw the dim white blur that indicated her face, and it was very dear to him, all of a sudden -- dearer, far, than he had ever realized.

"Good little girl!" he exclaimed, giving her the rifle. For a moment his hand pressed hers. Then with a quick intake of the breath, he strode over to the window and once more listened. She followed.

"Much nearer, now!" judged he. "Hear that, will you?"

Again they listened.

Louder now the drums sounded, dull, ominous, pulsating like the hammering of a fever-pulse inside a sick man's skull. A dull, confused hum, a noise as of a swarming mass of bees, drifted downwind.

"Maybe they'll pass by?" whispered Beatrice.

"It's Madison Forest they're aiming at!" returned the engineer. "See there!"

He pointed to westward.

There, far off along the forest-lane of Fourteenth Street, a sudden gleam of light flashed out among the trees, vanished, reappeared, was joined by two, ten, a hundred others. And now the whole approach to Madison Forest, by several streets, began to sparkle with these feux-follets, weaving and flickering unsteadily toward the square.

Here, there, everywhere through the dense masses of foliage, the watchers could already see a dim and moving mass, fitfully illuminated by torches that now burned steady, now flared into red and smoky tourbillons of flame in the night-wind.

"Like monster glow-worms, crawling among the trees!" the girl exclaimed. "We could mow them down, from here, already! God grant we sha'n't have to fight!"

"S-h-h-h! Wait and see what's up!"

Now, from the other horde, coming from the north, sounds of warlike preparation were growing ever louder.

With quicker beats the insistent tom-toms throbbed their

rhythmic melancholy rune, hollow and dissonant. Then all at once the drums ceased; and through the night air drifted a minor chant; a wail, that rose, fell, died, and came again as many strange voices joined it.

And from the square, below, a shrill, high-pitched, half-animal cry responded. Creeping shudders chilled the flesh along the engineer's backbone.

"What I need, now," thought he, "is about a hundred pounds of high-grade dynamite, or a gallon of nitroglycerin. Better still, a dozen capsules of my own invention, my 'Pulverite!'

"I guess that would settle things mighty quick. It would be the joker in this game, all right! Well, why not make some? With what chemicals I've got left, couldn't I work up a half-pint? Bottled in glass flasks, I guess it would turn the trick on 'em!"

"Why, they look black!" suddenly interrupted the girl. "See there -- and there?"

She pointed toward the spring. Stern saw moving shadows in the dark. Then, through an opening, he got a blurred impression of a hand, holding a torch. He saw a body, half-human.

The glimpse vanished, but he had seen enough.

"Black -- yes, blue-black! They seem so, anyhow. And -- why, did you see the size of them? No bigger than apes! Good Heaven!"

Involuntarily he shuddered. For now, like a dream-horde of hideous creatures seen in a nightmare, the torch-bearers had spread all through the forest at the base of the Metropolitan.

Away from the building out across by the spring and even to Fifth Avenue the mob extended, here thick, there thin, without order or coherence -- a shifting, murmuring, formless, seemingly planless congeries of dull brutality.

Here or there, where the swaying of the trees parted the branches a little, the wavering lights brought some fragment of the mass to view.

No white thing showed anywhere. All was dark and vague. Indistinctly, waveringly as in a vision, dusky heads could be made out. There showed a naked arm, greasily shining for a second in the ruddy glow which now diffused itself through the whole wood. Here the watchers saw a glistening back; again, an out-thrust leg, small and crooked, apelike and repulsive.

And once again the engineer got a glimpse of a misshapen hand, a long, lean, hideous hand that clutched a spear. But, hardly seen, it vanished into obscurity once more.

"Seems as though malformed human members, black and bestial, had been flung at random into a ghastly kaleidoscope, turned by a madman!" whispered Stern. The girl answering nothing, peered out in fascinated horror.

Up, up to the watchers rose a steady droning hum; and from the northward, ever louder, ever clearer, came now the war-song of the attacking party. The drums began again, suddenly. A high-pitched, screaming laugh echoed and died among the woods beyond the ruins of Twenty-eighth street.

Still in through the western approaches of the square, more and more lights kept straggling. Thicker and still more thick grew the press below. Now the torch-glow was strong enough to cast its lurid reflections on the vacant-staring wrecks of windows and of walls, gaping like the shattered skulls of a civilization which was no more. To the nostrils of the man and woman up floated an acrid, pitchy smell. And birds, dislodged from sleep, began to zigzag about, aimlessly, with frightened cries. One even dashed against the building, close at hand; and fell, a fluttering, broken thing, to earth.

Stern, with a word of hot anger, fingered his revolver. But Beatrice laid her hand upon his arm.

"Not yet!" begged she.

He glanced down at her, where she stood beside him at the empty embrasure of the window. The dim light from the vast and empty overarch of sky, powdered with a wonder of stars, showed him the vague outline of her face. Wistful and pale she was, yet very brave. Through Stern welled a sudden tenderness.

He put his arm around her, and for a moment her head lay on his breast.

But only a moment.

For, all at once, a snarling cry rang through the wood; and, with a northward surge of the torch-bearers, a confused tumult of shrieks, howls, simian chatterings and dull blows, the battle joined between those two vague, strange forces down below in the black forest.

17. Stern's Resolve

How long it lasted, what its meaning, its details, the watchers could not tell. Impossible, from that height and in that gloom, broken only by an occasional pale gleam of moonlight through the drifting cloud-rack, to judge the fortunes of this primitive war.

They knew not the point at issue nor yet the tide of victory or loss. Only they knew that back and forth the torches flared, the war-drums boomed and rattled, the yelling, slaughtering, demoniac hordes surged in a swirl of bestial murder-lust.

And so time passed, and fewer grew the drums, yet the torches flared on; and, as the first gray dawn went fingering up the sky there came a break, a flight, a merciless pursuit.

Dimly the man and woman, up aloft, saw things that ran and shrieked and were cut down -- saw things, there in the forest, that died even as they killed, and mingled the howl of triumph with the bubbling gasp of dissolution.

"Ugh! A beast war!" shuddered the engineer, at length, drawing Beatrice away from the window. "Come, it's getting light, again. It's too clear, now -- come away!"

She yielded, waking as it were from the horrid fascination that had held her spell-bound. Down she sat on her bed of furs, covered her eyes with her hands, and for a while remained quite motionless. Stern watched her. And again his hand sought the revolver-butt.

"I ought to have waded into that bunch, long ago," thought he. "We both ought to have. What it's all about, who could tell? But it's an outrage against the night itself, against the world, even dead though it be. If it hadn't been for wasting good ammunition for nothing -- !"

A curious, guttural whine, down there in the forest, attracted his attention. Over to the window he strode, and once again peered down.

A change had come upon the scene, a sudden, radical change. No more the sounds of combat rose; but now a dull, conclamant murmur as of victory and preparation for some ghastly rite.

Already in the center of the wood, hard by the spring, a little fire had been lighted. Even as Stern looked, dim, moving figures heaped on wood. The engineer saw whirling droves of sparks spiral upward; he saw dense smoke, followed by a larger flame.

And, grouped around this, already some hundreds of the now paling torches cast their livid glare.

Off to one side he could just distinguish what seemed to be a group engaged in some activity -- but what this might be, he could not determine. Yet, all at once a scream of pain burst out, therefrom; and then a gasping cry that ended quickly and did not come again.

Another shriek, and still a third; and now into the leaping flames some dark, misshapen things were flung, and a great shout arose.

Then rose, also, a shrill, singsong whine; and suddenly drums roared, now with a different cadence.

"Hark!" said the engineer. "The torchmen must have exterminated the other bunch, and got possession of the drums. They're using 'em, themselves -- and badly!"

By the firelight vague shapes came and went, their shadows grotesquely flung against the leafy screens. The figures quickened their paces and their gestures; then suddenly, with cries, flung themselves into wild activity. And all about the fire, Stern saw a wheeling, circling, eddying mob of black and frightful shapes.

"The swine!" he breathed. "Wait -- wait till I make a pint or two of Pulverite!"

Even as he spoke, the concourse grew quiet with expectancy. A silence fell upon the forest. Something was being led forward toward the fire -- something, for which the others all made way.

The wind freshened. With it, increased the volume of smoke.

Another frightened bird, cheeping forlornly, fluttered above the tree-tops.

Then rose a cry, a shriek long-drawn and ghastly, that climbed till it broke in a bubbling, choking gasp.

Came a sharp clicking sound, a quick scuffle, a grunt; then silence once more.

And all at once the drums crashed; and the dance began again, madder, more obscenely hideous than ever.

"Voodoo!" gulped Stern. "Obeah-work! And -- and the quicker I get my Pulverite to working, the better!"

Undecided no longer, determined now on a course of definite action without further delay, the engineer turned back into the room. Upon his forehead stood a cold and prickling sweat, of horror and disgust. But to his lips he forced a smile, as, in the half light of the red and windy dawn, he drew close to Beatrice.

Then all at once, to his unspeakable relief, he saw the girl was sleeping.

Utterly worn out, exhausted and spent with the long strain, the terrible fatigues of the past thirty-six hours, she had lain down and had dropped off to sleep. There she lay at full length. Very beautiful she looked, half seen in the morning gloom. One arm crossed her full bosom; the other pillowed her cheek. And, bending close, Stern watched her a long minute.

With strange emotion he heard her even breathing; he caught the perfume of her warm, ripe womanhood. Never had she seemed to him so perfect, so infinitely to be loved, to be desired.

And at thought of that beast-horde in the wood below, at realization of what might be, if they two should chance to be discovered and made captive, his face went hard as iron. An ugly, savage look possessed him, and he clenched both fists.

For a brief second he stooped still closer; he laid his lips soundlessly, gently upon her hair. And when again he stood up, the look in his eyes boded scant good to anything that might threaten the sleeping girl.

"So, now to work!" said he.

Into his own room he stepped quietly, his room where he had

collected his various implements and chemicals. First of all he set out, on the floor, a two-quart copper tea-kettle; and beside this, choosing carefully, he ranged the necessary ingredients for a "making" of his secret explosive.

"Now, the wash-out water," said he, taking another larger dish. Over to the water-pail he walked. Then he stopped, suddenly, frowning a black and puzzled frown.

"What?" he exclaimed. "But -- there isn't a pint left, all together! Hem! Now then, here is a situation."

Hastily he recalled how the great labors of the previous day, the wireless experiments and all, had prevented him from going out to the spring to replenish his supply. Now, though he bitterly cursed himself for his neglect, that did no good. The fact remained, there was no water.

"Scant pint, maybe!" said he. "And I've got to have a gallon, at the very least. To say nothing of drink for two people! And the horde, there, camping round the spring. Je-ru-salem!"

Softly he whistled to himself; then, trying to solve this vital, unexpected problem, fell to pacing the floor.

Day, slowly looming through the window, showed his features set and hard. Close at hand, the breath of morning winds stirred the treetops. But of the usual busy twitter and gossip of birds among the branches, now there was none. For down below there, in the forest, the ghoulish vampire revels still held sway.

Stern, at a loss, swore hotly under his breath.

Then suddenly he found himself; he came to a decision.

"I'm going down," he vowed. "I'm going down, to see!"

18. The Supreme Question

Now that his course lay clear before him, the man felt an instant and a huge relief. Whatever the risks, the dangers, this adventuring was better than a mere inaction, besieged there in the tower by that ugly, misshapen horde.

First of all, as he had done on the first morning of the awakening, when he had left the girl asleep, he wrote a brief communication to forestall any possible alarm on her part. This, scrawled with charcoal on a piece of smooth hide, ran:

"Have had to go down to get water and lay of the land. Absolutely necessary. Don't be afraid. Am between you and them, well armed. Will leave you both the rifle and the shotgun. Stay here, and have no fear. Will come back as soon as possible. Allan."

He laid this primitive letter where, on awakening, she could not fail to see it. Then, making sure again that all the arms were fully charged, he put the rifle and the gun close beside his "note," and saw to it that his revolvers lay loosely and conveniently in the holsters she had made for him.

One more reconnaissance he made at the front window. This done, he took the water-pail and set off quietly down the stairs. His feet were noiseless as a cat's.

At every landing he stopped, listening intently. Down, ever down, storey by storey he crept.

To his chagrin -- though he had half expected worse -- he found that the boiler-explosion of the previous night had really made the way impassible, from the third story downward. These lowest flights of steps had been so badly broken, that now they gave no access to the arcade.

All that remained of them was a jumbled mass of wreckage, below the gaping hole in the third-floor hallway.

"That means," said Stern to himself, "I've got to find another way down. And quick, too!"

He set about the task with a will. Exploration of several lateral corridors resulted in nothing; but at last good fortune led him to stairs that had remained comparatively uninjured. And down these he stole, pail in one hand, revolver ready in the other, listening, creeping, every sense alert.

He found himself, at length, in the shattered and dismembered wreckage of the once-famed "Marble Court." Fallen now were the carved and gilded pillars; gone, save here or there for a fragment, the wondrous balustrade. One of the huge newel-posts at the bottom lay on the cracked floor of marble squares; the other, its metal chandelier still clinging to it, lolled drunkenly askew.

But Stern had neither time nor inclination to observe these woful changes. Instead, he pressed still forward, and, after a certain time of effort, found himself in the arcade once more.

Here the effects of the explosion were very marked. A ghastly hole opened into the subcellar below; masses of fallen ceiling blocked the way; and every pane of glass in the shop-fronts had shattered down. Smoke had blackened everything. Ashes and dirt, ad infinitum, completed the dreary picture, seen there by the still insufficient light of morning.

But Stern cared nothing for all this. It even cheered him a trifle.

"In case of a mix-up," thought he, "there couldn't be a better place for ambushing these infernal cannibals -- for mowing them down, wholesale -- for sending them skyhooting to Tophet, in bunches!"

And with a grim smile, he worked his way cautiously toward Madison Forest and the pine-tree gate.

As he drew near, his care redoubled. His grip on the revolver-butt tightened.

"They mustn't see me -- first!" said he to himself.

Into a littered wreck of an office at the right of the exit he silently crept. Here, he knew, the outer wall of the building was deeply fissured. He hoped he might be able to find some peep-hole where, unseen, he could peer out on the bestial mob.

He set his water-pail down, and on hands and knees, hardly

breathing, taking infinite pains not to stir the loose rubbish on the floor, not even to crunch the fallen lumps of mortar, forward he crawled.

Yes, there was a glimmer of light through the crack in the wall. Stern silently wormed in between a corroded steel I-beam and a cracked granite block, about the edges of which the small green tendrils of a vine had laid their hold.

This way, then that, he craned his neck. And all at once, with a sharp breath, he grew rigid in horrified, eager attention.

"Great Lord!" he whispered. "What?"

Though, from the upper stories and by torch-light, he had already formed some notion of the Horde, he had in no wise been prepared for what he now was actually beholding through a screen of sumacs that grew along the wall outside.

"Why -- why, this can't be real!" thought he. "It -- must be some damned hallucination. Eh? Am I awake? What the deuce!"

Paling a little, his eyes staring, mouth agape, the engineer stayed there for a long minute unable to credit his own senses. For now he, he, the only white man living in the twenty-eighth century, was witnessing the strangest sight that ever a civilized being had looked upon in the whole history of the world.

No vision of DeQuincey, no drug-born dream of Poe could equal it for grisly fascination. Frankenstein, de Maupassant's "Horla," all the fantastic literary monsters of the past faded to tawdry, childish bogeys beside the actual observations of Stern, the engineer, the man of science and cold fact.

"Why -- what are these?" he asked himself, shuddering despite himself at the mere sight of what lay outside there in the forest. "What? Men? Animals? Neither! God help me, what -- what are these things?"

19. The Unknown Race

An almost irresistible repugnance, a compelling aversion, more of the spirit than of the flesh, instantly seized the man at sight of even the few members of the Horde which lay within his view.

Though he had been expecting to see something disgusting, something grotesque and horrible, his mind was wholly unprepared for the real hideousness of these creatures, now seen by the ever-strengthening light of day.

And slowly, as he stared, the knowledge dawned on him that here was a monstrous problem to face, far greater and more urgent than he had foreseen; here were factors not yet understood; here, the product of forces till then not even dreamed of by his scientific mind.

"I -- I certainly did expect to find a small race," thought he. "Small, and possibly misshapen, the descendants, maybe, of a few survivors of the cataclysm. But this -- !"

And again, fascinated by the ghastly spectacle, he laid his eye to the chink in the wall, and looked.

A tenuous fog still drifted slowly among the forest trees, veiling the deeper recesses. Yet, near at hand, within the limited segment of vision which the engineer commanded, everything could be made out with reasonable distinctness.

Some of the Things (for so he mentally named them, knowing no better term) were squatting, lying or moving about, quite close at hand. The fire by the spring had now almost died down. It was evident that the revel had ceased, and that the Horde was settling down to rest -- glutted, no doubt, with the raw and bleeding flesh of the conquered foe.

Stern could easily have poked his pistol muzzle through the

crack in the wall and shot down many of them. For an instant the temptation lay strong upon him to get rid of at least a dozen or a score; but prudence restrained his hand.

"No use!" he told himself. "Nothing to be gained by that. But, once I get my proper chance at them -- !"

And again, striving to observe them with the cool and calculating eye of science, he studied the shifting, confused picture out there before him.

Then he realized that the feature which, above all else, struck him as ghastly and unnatural, was the color of the Things.

"Not black, not even brown," said he. "I thought so, last night, but daylight corrects the impression. Not red, either, or coppercolored. What color, then? For Heaven's sake, what?"

He could hardly name it. Through the fog, it struck him as a dull slate-gray, almost a blue. He recalled that once he had seen a child's modeling-clay, much-used and very dirty, of the same shade, which certainly had no designation in the chromatic scale. Some of the Things were darker, some a trifle lighter -- these, no doubt, the younger ones -- but they all partook of this same characteristic tint. And the skin, moreover, looked dull and sickly, rather mottled and wholly repulsive, very like that of a Mexican dog.

Like that dog's hide, too, it was sparsely overgrown with whitish bristles. Here or there, on the bodies of some of the larger Things, bulbous warts had formed, somewhat like those on a toad's back; and on these warts the bristles clustered thickly. Stern saw the hair, on the neck of one of these creatures, crawl and rise like a jackal's, as a neighbor jostled him; and from the Thing's throat issued a clicking grunt of purely animal resentment.

"Merciful Heavens! What are they?" wondered Stern, again, utterly baffled for any explanation. "What can they be?"

Another, in the group close by, attracted his attention. It was lying on its side, asleep maybe, its back directly toward the engineer. Stern clearly saw the narrow shoulders and the thin, long arms, covered with that white bristling hair.

One sprawling, spatulate, clawlike hand lay on the forest moss. The twisted little apelike legs, disproportionately short, were curled up; the feet, prehensile and with a well-marked thumb on each, twitched a little now and then. The head, enormously too big for the body, to which it was joined by a thin neck, seemed to be scantily covered with a fine, curling down, of a dirty yellowish drab color.

"What a target!" thought the engineer. "At this distance, with my .38, I could drill it without half trying!"

All at once, another of the group sat up, shoved away a burned-out torch, and yawned with a noisy, doglike whine Stern got a quick yet definite glimpse of the sharp canine teeth; he saw that the Thing's fleshless lips and retreating chin were caked with dried blood. The tongue he saw was long and lithe and apparently rasped.

Then the creature stood up, balancing on its absurd bandy legs, a spear in its hand -- a flint-pointed spear of crude workmanship.

At full sight of the face, Stern shrank for a moment.

"I've known savages, as such," thought he. "I understand them. I know animals. They're animals, that's all. But this creature -- merciful Heaven!"

And at the realization that it was neither beast nor man, the engineer's blood chilled within his veins.

Yet he forced himself still to look and to observe, unseen. There was practically no forehead at all. The nose was but a formless lump of cartilage, the ears large and pendulous and hairy. Under heavy brow-ridges, the dull, lackluster eyes blinked stupidly, bloodshot and cruel. As the mouth closed, Stern noted how the under incisors closed up over the upper lip, showing a gleam of dull yellowish ivory; a slaver dripped from the doglike corner of the mouth.

Stern shivered, and drew back.

He realized now that he was in the presence of an unknown semi-human type, different in all probability from any that had ever yet existed. It was less their bestiality that disgusted him, than their utter, hopeless, age-long degeneration from the man-standard.

What race had they descended from? He could not tell. He thought he could detect a trace of the Mongol in the region of the eye, in the cheek-bones and the general contour of what, by courtesy, might be called the face. There were indications, also, of the negroid type, still stronger. But the color -- whence could that have come? And the general characteristics, were not these distinctly simian?

Again he looked. And now one of the pot-bellied little horrors, shambling and bulbous-kneed, was scratching its warty, blue hide with its black claws as it trailed along through the forest. It looked up, grinning and jabbering; Stern saw the teeth that should have been molars. With repulsion he noted that they were not flat-crowned, but sharp like a dog's. Through the blue lips they clearly showed.

"Nothing herbivorous here," thought the scientist. "All flesh -- food of -- who knows what sort!"

Quickly his mind ran over the outlines of the problem. He knew at once that these Things were lower than any human race ever recorded, far lower even than the famed Australian bushmen, who could not even count as high as five. Yet, strange and more than strange, they had the use of fire, of the tom-tom, of some sort of voodooism, of flint, of spears, and of a rude sort of tanning -- witness the loin-clouts of hide which they all wore.

"Worse than any troglodyte!" he told himself. "Far lower than De Quatrefage's Neanderthal man, to judge from the cephalic index -- worse than that Java skull, the pithecanthropus erectus, itself! And I am with my living eyes beholding them!"

A slight sound, there behind him in the room, set his heart flailing madly.

His hand froze to the butt of the automatic as he drew back from the cleft in the wall, and, staring, whirled about, ready to shoot on the second.

Then he started back. His jaw dropped, his eyes widened and limply fell his arm. The pistol swung loosely at his side.

"You? -- " he soundlessly breathed, "You -- here?"

There at the door of the great empty room, magnificent in her tiger-skin, the Krag gripped in her supple hand, stood Beatrice.

20. The Curiosity of Eve

At him the girl peered eagerly, a second, as though to make quite sure he was not hurt in any way, to satisfy herself that he was safe and sound.

Then with a little gasp of relief, she ran to him. Her sandaled feet lightly disturbed the rubbish on the floor; dust rose. Stern checked her with an upraised hand.

"Back! Back! Go back, quick!" he formed the words of command on his trembling lips. The idea of this girl's close proximity to the beast-horde terrified him, for the moment. "Back! What on earth are you here for?"

"I -- I woke up. I found you gone!" she whispered.

"Yes, but didn't you read my letter? This is no place for you!"

"I had to come! How could I stay up there, alone, when you -- were -- oh! maybe in danger -- maybe in need of me?"

"Come!" he commanded, in his perturbation heedless of the look she gave him. He took her hand. "Come, we must get out of this! It's too -- too near the -- "

"The what? What is it, Allan? Tell me, have you seen them? Do you know?"

Even excited as the engineer was, he realized that for the first time the girl had called him by his Christian name. Not even the perilous situation could stifle the thrill that ran through him at the sound of it. But all he answered was:

"No, I don't know what to call them. Have no idea, as yet. I've seen them, yes; but what they are, Heaven knows -- maybe!"

"Let me see, too!" she pleaded eagerly. "Is it through that crack in the wall? Is that the place to look?"

She moved toward it, her face blanched with excitement, eyes shining, lips parted. But Stern held her back. By the shoulder he took her.

"No, no, little girl!" he whispered. "You -- you mustn't! Really must not, you know. It's too awful!"

Up at him she looked, knowing not what to think or say for a moment. Their eyes met, there in that wrecked and riven place, lighted by the dull, misty, morning gray. Then Stern spoke, for in her gaze abode questions unnumbered.

"I'd much rather you wouldn't look out at them, not just yet," said he, speaking very low, fearful lest the murmur of his voice might penetrate the wall. "Just what they are, frankly, there's no telling."

"You mean -- ?"

"Come back into the arcade, where we'll be safer from discovery, and we can talk. Not here. Come!"

She obeyed. Together they retreated to the inner court.

"You see," he commented, nodding at the empty water-pail, "I haven't been to the spring yet. Not very likely to get there for a while, either, unless -- well, unless something pretty radical happens. I think these chaps have settled down for a good long stay in their happy hunting-ground, after the fight and the big feast. It's sort of a notion I've got, that this place, here, is some ancient, ceremonial ground of theirs."

"You mean, on account of the tower?"

He nodded.

"Yes, if they've got any religious ideas at all, or rather superstitions, such would very likely center round the most conspicuous object in their world. Probably the spring is a regular voodoo hangout. The row, last night, must have been a sort of periodic argument to see who was going to run the show."

"But," exclaimed the girl, in alarm -- "but if they do stay a while, what about us? We simply must have water!"

"True enough. And, inasmuch as we can't drink brine and don't know where there's any other spring, it looks as though we'd either have to make up to these fellows or wade into them, doesn't it? But we'll get water safe enough, never fear. Just now, for the immediate present, I want to get my bearings a little, before going to work. They seem to be resting up, a bit, after their pleasant little soirée. Now, if they'd only all go to sleep, it'd be a walk-over!"

The girl looked at him, very seriously.

"You mustn't go out there alone, whatever happens!" she exclaimed. "I just won't let you! But tell me," she questioned again, "how much have you really found out about them -- whatever they are."

"Not much. They seem to be part of a nomadic race of half-human things, that's about all I can tell as yet. Perhaps all the white and yellow peoples perished utterly in the cataclysm, leaving only a few scattered blacks. You know blacks are immune to several germ-infections that destroy other races."

"Yes. And you mean -- ?"

"It's quite possible these fellows are the far-distant and degenerate survivors of that other time."

"So the whole world may have gone to pieces the way Liberia and Haiti and Santo Domingo once did, when white rule ceased?"

"Yes, only a million times more so. I see you know your history! If my hypothesis is correct, and only a few thousand blacks escaped, you can easily imagine what must have happened."

"For a while, maybe fifty or a hundred years, they may have kept some sort of dwindling civilization. Probably the English language for a while continued, in ever more and more corrupt forms. There may have been some pretense of maintaining the school system, railroads, steamship lines, newspapers and churches, banks and all the rest of that wonderfully complex system we once knew. But after a while -- "

"Yes? What then?"

"Why, the whole false shell crumbled, that's all. It must have! History shows it. It didn't take a hundred years after Toussaint L'Ouverture and Dessalines, in Haiti, for the blacks to shuck off French civilization and go back to grass huts and human sacrifice -- to make another little Central Africa out of it, in the backwoods districts, at any rate. And we -- have had a thousand, Beatrice, since the white man died!"

She thought a moment, and shook her head.

"What a story," she murmured, "what an incredible, horribly fascinating story that would make, if it could ever be known, or written! Think of the ebb-tide of everything! Railroads abandoned and falling to pieces, cities crumbling, ships no longer sailing, language and arts and letters forgotten, agriculture shrinking back to a few patches of corn and potatoes, and then to nothing at all, everything changing, dying, stopping -- and the ever-increasing yet degenerating people leaving the city ruins, which they could not rebuild -- taking to the fields, the forests, the mountains -- going down, down, back toward the primeval state, down through barbarism, through savagery, to -- what?"

"To what we see!" answered the engineer, bitterly. "To animals, retaining by ghastly mockery some use of fire and of tools. All this, according to one theory."

"Is there another?" she asked eagerly.

"Yes, and I wish we had the shade of Darwin, of Haeckel or of Clodd here with us to help us work it out!"

"How do you imagine it?"

"Why, like this. Maybe, after all, even the entire black race was swept out along with the others, too. Perhaps you and I were really the only two human beings left alive in the world."

"Yes, but in that case, how -- ?"

"How came they here? Listen! May they not be the product of some entirely different process of development? May not some animal stock, under changed environment, have easily evolved them? May not some other semi-human or near-human race be now in process of arising, here on earth, eventually to conquer and subdue it all again?"

For a moment she made no answer. Her breath came a little quickly as she tried to grasp the full significance of this tremendous concept.

"In a million years, or so," the engineer continued, "may not the descendants of these things once more be men, or something very like them? In other words, aren't we possibly witnessing the recreation of the human type? Aren't these the real pithecanthropi erecti, rather than the brown-skinned, reddish-haired creatures of the biological text-books? There's our problem!"

She made no answer, but a sudden overmastering curiosity leaped into her eyes.

"Let me see them for myself! I must! I will!"

And before he could detain her, the girl had started back into the room whence they had come.

"No, no! No, Beatrice!" he whispered, but she paid no heed to him. Across the littered floor she made her way. And by the time Stern could reach her side, she had set her face to the long, crumbling crack in the wall and with a burning eagerness was peering out into the forest.

21. Eve Becomes an Amazon

Stern laid a hand on her shoulder, striving to draw her away. This spectacle, it seemed to him, was no fit sight for her to gaze on. But she shrugged her shoulders as if to say: "I'm not a child! I'm your equal, now, and I must see!" So the engineer desisted. And he, too, set his eye to the twisting aperture.

At sight of the narrow segment of forest visible through it, and of the several members of the Horde, a strong revulsion came upon him.

Up welled a deep-seated love for the memory of the race of men and women as they once had been -- the people of the other days. Stern almost seemed to behold them again, those tall, athletic, straight-limbed men; those lithe, deep-breasted women, fair-skinned and with luxuriant hair; all alike now plunged for a thousand years in the abyss of death and of eternal oblivion.

Never before had the engineer realized how dear, how infinitely close to him his own race had been. Never had he so admired its diverse types of force and beauty, as now, now when all were but a dream.

"Ugh!" thought he, disgusted beyond measure at the sight before him. "And all these things are just as much alike as so many ants in a hill! I question if they've got the reason and the socialized intelligence of ants!"

He heard the girl breathe quick, as she, too, watched what was going on outside. A certain change had taken place there. The mist had somewhat thinned away, blown by the freshening breeze through Madison Forest and by the higher-rising sun. Both watchers could new see further into the woods; and both perceived that the Horde was for the most part disposing itself to sleep.

Only a few vague, uncertain figures were now moving about, with a strangely unsteady gait, weak-kneed and simian.

In the nearest group, which Stern had already had a chance to study, all save one of the creatures had lain down. The man and woman could quite plainly hear the raucous and bestial snoring of some half-dozen of the gorged Things.

"Come away, you've seen enough, more than enough!" he whispered in the girl's ear.

She shook her head.

"No, no!" she answered, under her breath. "How horrible -- and yet, how wonderful!"

Then a misfortune happened; trivial yet how direly pregnant!

For Stern, trying to readjust his position, laid his right hand on the wall above his head.

A little fragment of loose marble, long since ready to fall, dislodged itself and bounced with a sharp click against the steel I-beam over which they were both peeking.

The sound, perhaps, was no greater than you would make in snapping an ordinary lead-pencil in your fingers; yet on the instant three of the Things raised their bulbous and exaggerated heads in an attitude of intense, suspicious listening. Plain to see that their senses, at least, excelled those of the human being, even as a dog's might.

The individual which, alone of them all, had been standing, wheeled suddenly round and made a step or two toward the building. Both watchers saw him with terrible distinctness, there among the sumacs and birches, with the beauty of which he made a shocking contrast.

Plain now was the simian aspect, plain the sidelong and uncertain gait, bent back and crooked legs, the long, pendulous arms and dully ferocious face.

And as the Thing listened, its hair bristling, it thrust its villainous, apelike head well forward. Open fell the mouth, revealing the dog-teeth and the blue, shriveled-looking gums.

A wrinkle creased the low, dull brow. Watching with horrified fascination, Stern and Beatrice beheld -- and heard -- the creature sniff the air, as though taking up some scent of danger or of the hunt.

Then up came the right arm; they saw the claw-hand with a spear, poise itself a moment. From the open mouth burst with astounding force and suddenness a snarling yowl, inarticulate, shrill, horrible beyond all thinking.

An instant agitation took place all through the forest. The watchers could see only a small, fan-like space of it -- and even this, only a few rods from the building -- yet by the confused, vague noise that began, they knew the alarm had been given to the whole Horde.

Here, there, the cry was repeated. A shifting, moving sound began. In the visible group, the Things were getting to their handlike feet, standing unsteadily on their loose-skinned, scaly legs, gawping about them, whining and clicking with disgusting sounds.

Sudden, numbing fear seized Beatrice. Now for the first time she realized the imminent peril; now she regretted her insistence on seeing the Horde at close range.

She turned, pale and shaken; and her trembling hand sought the engineer's.

He still, for a moment, kept his eye to the crack, fascinated by the very horror of the sight. Then all at once another figure shambled into view.

"A female one!" he realized, shuddering. Too monstrously hideous, this sight, to be endured. With a gasp, the man turned back.

About Beatrice he drew his arm. Together, almost as soundlessly as wraiths, they stole away, out through the office, out to the hallway, into the dim light of the arcade once more.

Here, for a few moments, they knew that they were safe. Retreat through the Marble Court and up the stairs was fairly clear. There was but one entrance open into the arcade, the one through Pine Tree Gate; and this was blocked so narrowly by the giant bole that Stern knew there could be no general mob-rush through it -- no attack which he could not for a while hold back, so long as his ammunition and the girl's should last.

Thus they breathed more freely now. Most of the tumult outside had been cut off from their hearing, by the retirement into the arcade. They paused, to plan their course.

At Stern the girl looked eagerly.

"Oh, oh, Allan -- how horrible!" she whispered. "It was all my fault for having been so headstrong, for having insisted on a look at them! Forgive me!"

"S-h-h-h!" he cautioned again. "No matter about that. The main thing, now, is whether we attack or wait?"

"Attack? Now?"

"I don't think much of going upstairs without that pail of water. We'll have a frightful time with thirst, to say nothing of not being able to make the Pulverite. Water we must have! If it weren't for your being here, I'd mighty soon wade into that bunch and see who wins! But -- well, I haven't any right to endanger -- "

Beatrice seized his hand and pulled him toward the doorway.

"Come on!" cried she. "If you and I aren't a match for them, we don't deserve to live, that's all. You know how I can shoot now! Come along!"

Her eyes gleamed with the light of battle, battle for liberty, for life; her cheeks glowed with the tides of generous blood that coursed beneath the skin. Never had Stern beheld her half so beautiful, so regal in that clinging, barbaric Bengal robe of black and yellow, caught at the throat with the clasp of raw gold.

A sudden impulse seized him, dominant, resistless. For a brief moment he detained her; he held her back; about her supple body his arm tightened.

She raised her face in wonder. He bent, a little, and on the brow he kissed her rapturously.

"Thank God for such a comrade and a -- friend!" said he.

22. Gods!

Some few minutes later, together they approached Pine Tree Gate, leading directly out into the Horde.

The girl, rosier than ever, held her Krag loosely in the hollow of her bare, warm right arm. One of Stern's revolvers lay in its holster. The other balanced itself in his right hand. His left held the precious water-pail, so vital now to all their plans and hopes.

Girt in his garb of fur, belted and sandaled, well over six feet tall and broad of shoulder, the man was magnificent. His red beard and mustache, close-cropped, gave him a savage air that now well fitted him. For Stern was mad -- mad clear through.

That Beatrice should suffer in any way, even from temporary thirst, raised up a savage resentment in his breast. The thought that perhaps it might not be possible to gain access to the spring at all, that these foul Things might try to blockade them and siege them to death, wrought powerfully on him.

For himself he cared nothing. The girl it was who now preoccupied his every thought. And as they made their way through the litter of the explosion, toward the exit, slowly and cautiously, he spied out every foot of the place for possible danger.

If fight he must, he knew now it would be a brutal, utterly merciless fight -- slaughter, extermination without any limit, to the end.

But there was scant time for thought. Already they could see daylight glimmering in through the gate, past the massive column of the conifer. Daylight -- and with it came a thin and acrid smoke -- and sounds of the uproused Horde in Madison Forest.

"Slow! Slow, now!" whispered Stern. "Don't let 'em know a thing until we've got 'em covered! If we surprise 'em just right, who knows but the whole infernal mob may duck and run? Don't shoot till you have to; but when you do -- !"

"I know!" breathed she.

Then, all at once, there they were at the gate, at the big tree, standing out there in the open, on the thick carpet of pine-spills.

And before them lay the mossy, shaded forest aisles -- with what a horror camped all through that peaceful, wondrous place!

"Oh!" gasped Beatrice. The engineer stopped as though frozen. His hand tightened on the revolver-butt till the knuckles whitened. And thus, face to face with the Horde, they stood for a long minute.

Neither of them realized exactly the details of that first impression. The narrow slit of view which they had already got through the crack in the wall had only very imperfectly prepared them for any understanding of what these Things really were, en masse.

But both Beatrice and the engineer understood, even at the first moment of their exit there, that they had entered an adventure whereof the end could not be foreseen; that here before them lay possibilities infinitely more serious than any they had contemplated.

For one thing, they had underestimated the numbers of the Horde. They had thought, perhaps, there might be five hundred in all.

The torches had certainly numbered no more than that. But now they realized that the torch-bearers had been but a very small fraction of the whole; for, as their eyes swept out through the forest, whence the fog had almost wholly risen, they beheld a moving, swarming mass of the creatures on every hand. A mass that seemed to extend on, on to indefinite vistas. A mass that moved, clicked, shifted, grunted, stank, snarled, quarreled. A mass of frightful hideousness, of inconceivable menace.

The girl's first impulse was to turn, to retreat back into the building once more; but her native courage checked it. For Stern, she saw, had no such purpose.

Surprised though he was, he stood there like a rock, head up, revolver ready, every muscle tense and ready for whatsoever might befall. And through the girl flashed a thrill of admiration for this virile, indomitable man, coping with every difficulty, facing every peril -- for her sake.

Yet the words he uttered now were not of classic heroism. They were simple, colloquial, inelegant. For Stern, his eyes blazing, said only:

"We're in bad, girl! They're on -- we've got to bluff -- bluff like the devil!"

Have you ever seen a herd of cattle on the prairie, a herd of thousands, shift and face and, as by instinct, lower their horned heads against some enemy -- a wolf-pack, maybe?

You know then, how this Horde of dwarfish, blue, warty, misformed little horrors woke to the presence of the unknown enemy.

Already half alarmed by the warning given by the one, which, near the crack in the wall, had sniffed the intruders and had howled, the pack now broke into commotion. Stern and Beatrice saw a confused upheaving, a shifting and a tumult. They heard a yapping outcry. The long, thin spears began to bristle.

And all at once, as a dull, ugly hornet-hum rose through the wood, they knew the moment for quick action was upon them.

"Here goes!" cried Stern, raging. "Let's see how this will strike the hell-hounds!"

His face white with passion and with loathing hate, he raised the automatic. He aimed at none of the pack, for angry as he was he realized that the time was not yet come for killing, if other means to reach the spring could possibly avail.

Instead he pointed the ugly blue muzzle up toward the branches of a maple, under which a dense swarm of the Horde had encamped and now was staring, apelike, at him.

Then his finger sought the trigger. And five crackling spurts of flame, five shots spat out into the calm and misty air of morning. A few severed leaves swayed down, idly, with a swinging motion. A broken twig fell, hung suspended a moment, then detached itself again and crapped to earth.

"Good Lord! Look a' that, will you?" cried Stern.

A startled cry broke from the girl's lips.

Both of them had expected some effect from the sudden fusillade, but nothing like that which actually resulted.

For, as the quick shots echoed to stillness again, and even before the first of the falling leaves had spiraled to the ground, an absolute, unbroken silence fell upon that vile rabble of beast-men -- the silence of a numbing, paralyzing, sheer brute terror.

Some stood motionless, crouching on their bandy legs, holding to whatsoever tree or bush was nearest, staring with wild eyes.

Others dropped to their knees.

But by far the greater part, thousands on thousands of the little monstrosities, fell prone and grovelling. Their hideous mask-like faces hidden, there they lay on the moss and all among the undergrowth, the trampled, desecrated, befouled undergrowth of Madison Forest.

Then all at once, over and beyond them, Stern saw the blue-curling smudge of the remains of the great fire by the spring.

He knew that, for a few brief, all-precious moments, the way might possibly be clear to come and go -- to get water -- to save Beatrice and himself from the thirst -- tortures -- to procure the one necessary thing for the making of his Pulverite.

His heart gave a great, up-bounding leap.

"Look, Beatrice!" cried he, his voice ringing out over the terror-stricken things. "Look -- we're gods! While this lasts -- gods! Come, now's our only chance! Come on! -- "

23. The Obeah

Together, as in a dream -- a nightmare, dazed, incredible, grotesque -- they advanced out into the dim-shaded forest aisles.

"Don't look!" Stern exclaimed, shuddering at sight of the unspeakable hideousness of the Things, at glimpses of gnawed bones, grisly bits of flesh, dried gouts of blood upon the woodland carpet. "Don't think -- just come along!

"Five minutes, and we're safe, there and back again. S-h-h-h! Don't hurry! Count, now -- count your steps -- one, two, three -- four, five, six -- steady, steady! -- "

Now they were ten yards from the tower, now twenty. Bravely they walked, now straight ahead among the trees, now circling some individual, some horrid group. Stern held the water-pail firmly. He gripped the revolver in a grasp of iron. The magazine-rifle lay in both the girl's hands, ready for instant use.

Suddenly Stern fired again, three shots.

"Some of 'em are moving, over there!" he said in a crisp, ugly tone. "I guess a little lead close to their ears will fix 'em for a while!"

His voice went to a hoarse whisper.

"Gods!" he repeated. "Don't forget it, for a moment; don't lose that thought, for it may pull us through! These creatures here, if they're descended from the blacks, must have some story, some tradition of the white man. Of his mastery, his power! We'll use it now, by Heaven, as it never yet was used!"

Then he began to count again; and so, tense, watching with eager-burning eyes and taut muscles, the man and woman made their way of frightful peril.

A snuffling howl rose.

"You will, will you?" Stern cried, adding another kick to the one he had just dealt to one of the creatures, who had ventured to look up at their approach. "Lie down, ape!" And with the clangorous metal pail he smote the ugly, brutish skull.

Beatrice gasped with fear; but the bluff made good. The creature grovelled, and again the pair strode forward, masterfully. Masterfully they had to go, or not at all. Masterfully, or die. For now their all-in-all lay just in that grim, steel-hard sense of mastery.

Before the girl's eyes a sort of haze seemed forming. Her heart beat thick and heavy. Stern's counting sounded very far away and strange; she hardly recognized his voice. To her came wild, disjointed, confused impressions -- now a bony and distorted back, now a simian head; again a group that crouched and cowered in its filthy squalor, hideously.

Then all at once, there right before her she saw the little woodland path that, slightly descending, led past a big oak she well knew, down to the margin of the pool.

"Steady, girl, steady!" came the engineer's warning, tense as piano-wire. "Almost there, now. What's that?"

For a brief instant he hesitated. The girl felt his arm grow even more taut, she heard his breath catch. Then she, too, looked -- and saw.

It was enough, that sight, to have smitten with sick horror the bravest man who ever lived. For there, beside the smouldering embers of the great feast-fire, littered with bones and indescribable refuse, a creature was squatting on its hams -- one of the Horde, indeed, yet vastly different, tremendously more venomous, more dangerous of aspect.

Stern knew at once that here, not prostrate nor yet crouching, was the chief of the blue Horde.

He knew it by the superior size and strength of the Thing, by the almost manlike cunning of the low, gorilla face, the gleam of intelligence in the reddened eye, the crude wreath of maple-leaves upon the head, the necklace of finger-bones strung around the neck.

But most of all, he knew it by a thing that shocked him more than the sight of stark, outright cannibalism would have done. A simple thing, yet how ominous! A thing that argued reason in this reversion from the human; a thing that sent the shuddering chills along the engineer's spine.

For the chief, the obeah-man of this vile drove, rising now from beside the fire with a gibbering chatter and a look of bestial malice, held between his fangs a twisted brown leaf.

Stern knew at a glance the leaf was the rudely cured product of some degenerate tobacco-plant. He saw a glow of red at the tip of the close-rolled tobacco. Vapor issued from the chief's slit-mouth.

"Good Lord -- he's -- smoking!" stammered the engineer. "And that means -- means an almost human brain. And -- quick, Beatrice, the water! I didn't expect this! Thought they were all alike. Back to the tower, quick! Here, fill the pail -- I'll keep him covered!"

Up he brought the automatic, till the bead lay fair upon the naked, muscular breast of the obeah.

Beatrice handed Stern the rifle, then snatching the pail, dipped it, filled it to the brim. Stern heard the water lap and gurgle. He knew it was but a few seconds, yet it seemed an hour to him, at the very least.

Keener than ever before in his whole life, his mental pictures now limned themselves with lightning rapidity upon his brain.

Stamped on his consciousness was this lithe, lean, formidable body, showing beyond dispute its human ancestry; the right hand that held a steel-pointed spear; the horrible ornament (a withered little smoked hand) that dangled from the left wrist by a cord of platted fiber.

Vividly Stern beheld a deep gash or scar that ran from the chief's right eye -- a dull, fishlike eye, evidently destroyed by that wound -- down across the leathery cheek, across the prognathous jaw; a reddish-purple wale, which on that clay-blue skin produced an effect indescribably repulsive.

Then the chief grunted, and moved forward, toward them. Stern saw that the gait was almost human, not shuffling and uncertain like that of the others, but firm and vigorous. He estimated the height at more than five feet, eight inches; the weight at possibly one hundred and forty pounds. Even at that juncture, his scientific mind, always accustomed to judging, instinctively registered these data, with the others.

"Here, you, get back there!" shouted Stern, as the girl rose again from filling the pail.

The cry was instinctive, for even as he uttered it, he knew it could not be understood. A thousand years of rapid degeneration had long wiped all traces of English speech from the brute-men, who now, at most, chattered some bestial gibberish. Yet the warning echoed loudly through Madison Forest; and the obeah hesitated.

The tone, perhaps, conveyed some meaning to that brain behind the sloping forehead. Perhaps some dim, racial memory of human speech still lingered in that mind, in that strange organism which, by some freak of atavism, had "thrown back" out of the mire of returning animality almost to the human form and stature once again.

However that may have been, the creature-chief halted in his advance. Undecided he stood a moment, leaning upon his spear, sucking at the rude mockery of a cigar. Stern remembered having seen Consul, the trained chimpanzee, smoke in precisely the same manner, and a nameless loathing filled him at his mockery of the dead, buried past.

"Let me carry the pail!" said he. "We've got to hurry -- hurry -- or it may be too late!"

"No, no -- I'll keep the water!" she answered, panting. "You need both hands clear! Come!"

Thus they turned, and, with a shuddering glance behind, started back for the tower again.

But the obeah, with a whining plaint, spat away his tobacco-leaf. They heard a shuffle of feet. And, looking round again, both saw that he had crossed the little brook.

There he stood now, his right hand out, palm upward, his lips curled in the ghastly imitation of a smile, blue gums and yellow lushes showing, a sight to freeze the blood with horror. Yet through it all, the meaning was most clearly evident.

Beatrice, laden as she was with the heavy water-bucket, more precious now to them than all the wealth of the dead world, would still have retreated, but with a word of stern command he bade her wait. He stopped short in his tracks.

"Not a step!" commanded he. "Hold on! If he makes friends with us -- with gods -- that's a million times better every way! Hold on -- wait, no -- this is his move."

He faced the obeah. His left hand gripped the repeating rifle, his right the automatic, held in readiness for instant action. The muzzle sight never for a second left its aim at the chief's heart.

And for a second silence fell there in the forest. Save for the rustling murmur of the Horde, and a faint, woodland trickle of the stream, you might have thought the place untouched by life.

Yet death lurked there, and destiny -- the destiny of the whole world, the future, the human race, forever and ever without end; and the cords of Fate were being loosed for a new knitting.

And Stern, with Beatrice there at his side, stood harsh and strong and very grim; stood like an incarnation of man's life, waiting.

And slowly, step by step, over the yielding, noiseless moss, the grinning, one-eyed, ghastly obeah-man came nearer, nearer still.

24. The Fight in the Forest

Now the Thing was close, very close to them, while a hush lay upon the watching Horde and on the forest. So close, that Stern could hear the soughing breath between those hideous lips and see the twitching of the wrinkled lid over the black, glittering eye that blinked as you have often seen a chimpanzee's.

All at once the obeah stopped. Stopped and leered, his head craned forward, that ghastly rictus on his mouth.

Stern's hot anger welled up again. Thus to be detained, inspected and seemingly made mock of by a creature no more than three-quarters human, stung the engineer to rage.

"What do you want?" cried he, in a thick and unsteady voice. "Anything I can do for you? If not, I'll be going."

The creature shook its head. Yet something of Stern's meaning may have won to its smoldering intelligence. For now it raised a hand. It pointed to the pail of water, then to its own mouth; again it indicated the pail, then stretched a long, repulsive finger at the mouth of Stern.

The meaning seemed clear. Stern, even as he stood there in anger -- and in wonder, too, at the fearlessness of this superthing -- grasped the significance of the action.

"Why, he must mean," said he, to Beatrice, "he must be trying to ask whether we intend to drink any of the water, what? Maybe it's poisoned, now, or something! Maybe he's trying to warn us!"

"Warn us? Why should he?"

"How can I tell? It isn't entirely impossible that he still retains some knowledge of his human ancestors. Perhaps that tradition may have been handed down, some way, and still exists in the form of a crude beast-religion."

"Yes, but then -- ?"

"Perhaps he wants to get in touch with us, again; learn from us; try to struggle up out of the mire of degeneration, who knows? If so -- and it's possible -- of course he'd try to warn us of a poisoned spring!"

Acting on this hypothesis, of which he was now half-convinced, Stern nodded. By gesture-play he answered: Yes. Yes, this woman and he intended to drink of the water. The obeah-man, grinning, showed signs of lively interest. His eyes brightened, and a look of craft, of wizened cunning crept over his uncanny features.

Then he raised his head and gave a long, shrill, throaty call, ululating and unspeakably weird.

Something stirred in the forest. Stern heard a rustle and a creeping murmur; and quick fear chilled his heart.

To him it seemed as though a voice were calling, perhaps the inner, secret voice of his own subjective self -- a voice that cried:

"You, who must drink water -- now he knows you are not gods, but mortal creatures. Tricked by his question and your answer, your peril now is on you! Flee!"

The voice died. Stern found himself, with a strange, taut eagerness tingling all through him, facing the obeah and -- and not daring to turn his back.

Retreat they must, he knew. Retreat, at once! Already in the forest he understood that heads were being lifted, beastlike ears were listening, brute eyes peering and ape-hands clutching the little, flint-pointed spears. Already the girl and he should have been half-way back to the tower; yet still, inhibited by that slow, grinning, staring advance of the chief, there the engineer stood.

But all at once the spell was broken.

For with a cry, a hoarse and frightful yell of passion, the obeah leaped -- leaped like a huge and frightfully agile ape -- leaped the whole distance intervening.

Stern saw the Thing's red-gleaming eyes fixed on Beatrice. In those eyes he clearly saw the hell-flame of lust. And as the woman screamed in terror, Stern pulled trigger with a savage curse.

The shot went wild. For at the instant -- though he felt no pain -- his arm dropped down and sideways.

Astounded, he looked. Something was wrong! What? His trigger-finger refused to serve. It had lost all power, all control.

For God's sake, what could it be?

Then -- all this taking but a second -- Stern saw; he knew the truth. Staring, pale and horrified, he understood.

There, through the fleshy part of his forearm, thrust clean from side to side by a lightning-swift stroke, he saw the obeah's spear!

It dangled strangely in the firm muscles. The steel barb and full eighteen inches of the shaft were red and dripping.

Yet still the engineer felt no slightest twinge of pain.

From his numbed, paralyzed hand the automatic dropped, fell noiselessly into the moss.

And with a formless roar of killing-rage, Stern swung on the obeah, with the rifle.

Stern felt his heart about to burst with hate. He did not even think of the second revolver in the holster at his side. With only his left hand now to use, the weapon could only have given clumsy service.

Instead, the man reverted instantly to the jungle stage, himself -- to the law of claw and fang, of clutching talon, of stone and club.

The beloved woman's cry, ringing in his ears, drove him mad. Up he whirled the Krag again, up, up, by the muzzle; and down upon that villainous skull he dashed it with a force that would have brained an ox.

The obeah, screeching, reeled back. But he was not dead. Not dead, only stunned a moment. And Stern, horrified, found himself holding only a gun-barrel. The stock, shattered, had whirled away and vanished among the tall and waving ferns.

Beatrice snatched up the fallen revolver. She stumbled; and the pail was empty. Spurting, splashing away, the precious water flew. No time, now, for any more.

For all about them, behind them and on every hand, the Things were closing in.

They had seen blood -- had heard the obeah's cry; they knew! Not gods, now, but mortal creatures! Not gods!

"Run! Run!" gasped Beatrice.

The spear still hanging from his arm, Stern wheeled and followed. High and hard he swung the rifle-barrel, like a war-club.

No counting of steps, now; no play at divinity. Panting, horror-stricken, frenzied with rage, bleeding, they ran. It was a hunt -- the hunt of the last two humans by the nightmare Horde.

In front, a bluish and confused mass seemed to dance and quiver through the forest; and a pattering rain of spears and little arrows began to fall about the fugitives.

Then the girl's revolver sputtered in a quick volley; and again, for a space, silence fell. The way again was clear. But in the path, silent and still, or writhing horribly, lay a few of the Things. And the pine-needles and soft moss were very red, in spots.

Stern had his pistol out too, by now. For behind and on his flanks, like ferrets hanging to a hunted creature, the swarm was closing in.

The engineer, his face very white and drawn, veins standing out on his sweat-beaded forehead, heard Beatrice cry out to him, but he could not understand her words.

Yet as they ran, he saw her level the pistol and snap the hammer twice, thrice, with no result. The little dead click sounded like a death-warrant to him.

"Empty?" cried he. "Here, take this one! You can shoot better now than I can!" And into her hand he thrust the second revolver.

Something stung him on the left shoulder. He glanced round. A dart was hanging there.

With an oath, the engineer wheeled about. His eyes burned and his lips drew back, taut, from his fine white teeth.

There, already recovered from the blow which would have killed a man ten times over, he saw the obeah snarling after him. Right down along the path the monster was howling, beating his breast with both huge fists. And, now feeling fear no more than pain, Stern crouched to meet his onslaught.

25. The Goal, and Through It

It all happened in a moment of time, a moment, long -- in seeming -- as an hour. The girl's revolver crackled, there behind him. Stern saw a little round bluish hole take shape in the obeah's ear, and red drops start.

Then with a ghastly screaming, the Thing was upon him.

Out struck the engineer, with the rifle-barrel. All the force of his splendid muscles lay behind that blow. The Thing tried to dodge. But Stern had been too quick.

Even as it sprang, with talons clutching for the man's throat, the steel barrel drove home on the jaw.

An unearthly, piercing yell split the forest air. Then Stern saw the obeah, his jaw hanging oddly awry, all loose and shattered, fall headlong in the path.

But before he could strike again, could batter in the base of the tough skull, a moan from Beatrice sent him to her aid.

"Oh, God!" he cried, and sank beside her on his knees.

On her forehead, as she lay gasping among the bushes, he saw an ugly welt.

"A stone? They've hit her with a stone! Killed her, perhaps?"

Kneeling there, up he snatched the revolver, and in a deadly fire he poured out the last spitting shots, pointblank in the faces of the crowding rabble.

Up he leaped. The rifle barrel flashed and glittered as he whirled it. Like a reaper, laying a clean swath behind him, the engineer mowed down a dozen of the beast-men.

Shrieks, grunts, snarls, mingled with his execrations.

Then fair into a jabbering ape-face he flung the bloodstained barrel. The face fell, faded, vanished, as hideous illusions fade in a dream.

And Stern, with a strength he never dreamed was his, caught up the fainting girl in his left arm, as easily as though she had been a child.

Still dragging the spear which pierced his right arm -- his right arm that yet protected her a little -- he ran.

Stones, darts, spears, clattered in about him. He heard the swish and tang of them; heard the leaves flutter as the missiles whirled through.

Struck? Was he struck again?

He knew not, nor cared. Only he thought of shielding Beatrice. Nothing but that, just that!

"The gate -- oh, let me reach the gate! God! The gate -- "

And all of a sudden, though how he could not tell, there he seemed to see the gate before him. Could it be? Or was that, too, a dream? A cruel, vicious mockery of his disordered mind?

Yes -- the gate! It must be! He recognized the giant pine, in a moment of lucidity. Then everything began to dance again, to quiver in the mocking sunlight.

"The gate!" he gasped once more, and staggered on. Behind him, a little trail of blood-drops from his wounded arm fell on the trampled leaves.

Something struck his bent head. Through it a blinding pain darted. Thousands of beautiful and tiny lights of every color began to quiver, to leap and whirl.

"They've -- set the building on fire!" thought he; yet all the while he knew it was impossible, he understood it was only an illusion.

He heard the rustle of the wind through the forest. It blended and mingled with a horrid tumult of grunts, of clicking cries, of gnashing teeth and little bestial cries.

"The -- gate!" sobbed Stern, between hard-set teeth, and stumbled forward, ever forward, through the Horde.

To him, protectingly, he clasped the beautiful body in the tiger-skin.

Living? Was she living yet? A great, aching wonder filled him.

Could he reach the stair with her, and bear her up it? Hurl back these devils? Save her, after all?

The pain had grown exquisite, in his head. Something seemed hammering there, with regular strokes -- a red-hot sledge upon an anvil of white-hot steel.

To him it looked as though a hundred, a thousand of the little blue fiends were leaping, shrieking, circling there in front of him. Ten thousand! And he must break through.

Break through!

Where had he heard those words? Ah -- Yes --

To him instantly recurred a distant echo of a song, a Harvard football-song. He remembered. Now he was back again. Yale, 0; Harvard, 17 -- New Haven, 1898. And see the thousands of cheering spectators! The hats flying through the air -- flags waving -- red, most of them! Crimson -- like blood!

Came the crash and boom of the old Harvard Band, with big Joe Foley banging the drum till it was fit to burst, with Marsh blowing his lungs out on the cornet, and all the other fellows raising Cain.

Uproar! Cheering! And again the music. Everybody was singing now, everybody roaring out that brave old fighting chorus:

"......Now -- all to-geth-er,
Smash them -- and -- break -- through!"

And see! Look there! The goal!

The scene shifted, all at once, in a quite unaccountable and puzzling manner.

Somehow, victory wasn't quite won, after all. Not quite yet. What was the matter, then? What was wrong? Where was he?

Ah, the Goal!

Yes, there through the rack and mass of the Blues, he saw it, again, quite clearly. He was sure of that, anyhow.

The goal-posts seemed a trifle near together, and they were certainly made of crumbling stone, instead of straight wooden beams. Odd, that!

He wondered, too, why the management allowed trees to grow on the field, trees and bushes -- why a huge pine should be standing right there by the left-hand post. That was certainly a matter to be investigated and complained of, later. But now was no time for kicks.

"Probably some Blue trick," thought Stern. "No matter, it won't do 'em any good, this time!"

Ah! An opening! Stern's head went lower still. He braced himself for a leap.

"Come on, come on!" he yelled defiance.

Again he heard the cheering, once wind like a chorus of mad devils.

An opening? No, he was mistaken. Instead, the Blues were massing there by the Goal.

Bitterly he swore. Under his arm he tightened the ball. He ran! What?

They were trying to tackle?

"Damn you!" he cried, in boiling anger. "I'll -- I'll show you a trick or two -- yet!"

He stopped, circled, dodged the clutching hands, feinted with a tactic long unthought of, and broke into a straight, resistless dash for the posts.

As he ran, he yelled:

"Smash them -- and -- break through! . ....."

All his waning strength upgathered for that run. Yet how strangely tired he felt -- how heavy the ball was growing!

What was the matter with his head? With his right arm? They both ached hideously. He must have got hurt, some way, in one of the "downs." Some dirty work, somewhere. Rotten sport!

He ran. Never in all his many games had he seen such peculiar gridiron, all tangled and overgrown. Never, such host of tackles. Hundreds of them! Where were the Crimsons? What? No support, no interference? Hell!

Yet the Goal was surely just there, now right ahead. He ran.

"Foul!" he shouted savagely, as a Blue struck at him, then another and another, and many more. The taste of blood came to his tongue. He spat. "Foul!"

Right and left he dashed them, with a giant's strength. They scattered in panic, with strange and unintelligible cries.

"The goal!"

He reached it. And, as he crossed the line, he fell.

"Down, down!" sobbed he.

26. Beatrice Dares

An hour later, Stern and Beatrice sat weak and shaken in their stronghold on the fifth floor, resting, trying to gather up some strength again, to pull together for resistance to the siege that had set in.

With the return of reason to the engineer -- his free bleeding had somewhat checked the onset of fever -- and of consciousness to the girl, they began to piece out, bit by bit, the stages of their retreat.

Now that Stern had barricaded the stairs, two stories below, and that for a little while they felt reasonably safe, they were able to take their bearings, to recall the flight, to plan a bit for the future, a future dark with menace, seemingly hopeless in its outlook.

"If it -- hadn't been for you," Beatrice was saying, "if you hadn't picked me up and carried me, when that stone struck, I -- I -- "

"How's the ache now?" Stern hastily interrupted, in a rather weak yet brisk voice, which he was trying hard to render matter-of-fact. "Of course the lack of water, except that half-pint or so, to bathe your bruise with, is a rank barbarity. But if we haven't got any, we haven't -- that's all. All -- till we have another go at 'em!"

"Oh, Allan!" she exclaimed, tremulously. "Don't think of me! Of me, when your back's gashed with a spear-cut, your head's battered, arm pierced, and we've neither water nor bandages -- nothing of any kind to treat your wounds with!"

"Come now, don't you bother about me!" he objected trying hard to smile, though racked with pain. "I'll be O. K., fit as a fiddle, in no time. Perfect health and all that sort of thing, you know. It'll heal right away.

"Head's clear again already, in spite of that whack with the war-club, or whatever it was they landed with. But for a while I certainly was seeing things. I had 'em -- had 'em bad! Thought -- well, strange things.

"My back? Only a scratch, that's all. It's begun to coagulate already, the blood has, hasn't it?" And he strove to peer over his own shoulder at the slash. But the pain made him desist. He could hardly keep back a groan. His face twitched involuntarily.

The girl sank on her knees beside him. Her arm encircled him; her hand smoothed his forehead; and with a strange look she studied his unnaturally pale face.

"It's your arm I'm thinking about, more than anything," said she. "We've got to have something to treat that with. Tell me, does it hurt you very much, Allan?"

He tried to laugh, as he glanced down at the wounded arm, which, ligatured about the spear-thrust with a thong, and supported by a rawhide sling, looked strangely blue and swollen.

"Hurt me? Nonsense! I'll be fine and dandy in no time. The only trouble is, I'm not much good as a fighter this way. Southpaw, you see. Can't shoot worth a -- a cent, you know, with my left. Otherwise, I wouldn't mind."

"Shoot? Trust me for that now!" she exclaimed. "We've still got two revolvers and the shotgun left, and lots of ammunition. I'll do the shooting -- if there's got to be any done!"

"You're all right, Beatrice!" exclaimed the wounded man fervently. "What would I do without you? And to think how near you came to -- but never mind. That's over now; forget it!"

"Yes, but what next?"

"Don't know. Get well, maybe. Things might be worse. I might have a broken arm, or something; laid up for weeks -- slow starvation and all that. What's a mere puncture? Nothing! Now that the spear's out, it'll begin healing right away.

"Bet a million, though, that What's-His-Name down there, Big Chief the Monk, won't get out of his scrape in a hurry. His face is certainly scrambled, or I miss my guess. You got him through the ear with one shot, by the way. Know that? Fact! Drilled it clean! Just a little to the right and you'd have had him for keeps. But never mind, we'll save him for the encore -- if there is any."

"You think they'll try again?"

"Can't say. They've lost a lot of fighters, killed and wounded, already. And they've had a pretty liberal taste of our style. That ought to hold them for a while! We'll see, at any rate. And if luck stays good, we'll maybe have a thing or two to show them if they keep on hanging round where they aren't wanted!"

Came now a little silence. Beside Stern the girl sat, half supporting his wounded body with her firm, white arm. Thirst was beginning to torment them both, particularly Stern, whose injuries had already given him a marked temperature. But water there was absolutely none. And so, still planless, glad only to recuperate a little, content that for the present the Horde had been held back, they waited. Waiting, they both thought. The girl's thoughts were all of him; but he, man-fashion, was trying to piece out what had happened, to frame some coherent idea of it all, to analyze the urgent necessities that lay upon them both.

Here and there, a disjointed bit recurred to him, even from out of the delirium that had followed the blow on the head. From the time he had recovered his senses in the building, things were clearer.

He knew that the Horde, temporarily frightened by his mad rush, had given him time to stumble up again and once more lift the girl, before they had ventured to creep into the arcade in search of their prey.

He remembered that the spear had been gone then. Raving, he must have broken and plucked it out. The blood, he recalled, was spurting freely as he had carried Beatrice through the wreckage and up to the first landing, where she had regained partial consciousness.

Then he shuddered at recollection of that stealthy, apelike creeping of the Horde scouts in among the ruins, furtive and silent; their sniffing after the blood-track; their frightful agility in clambering with feet and hands alike, swinging themselves up like chimpanzees, swarming aloft on the death-hunt.

He had evaded them, from storey to storey. Beatrice, able now to walk, had helped him roll down balustrades and building-stones, fling rocks, wrench stairs loose and block the way.

And so, wounding their pursuers, yet tracked always by more and ever more, they had come to the landing, where by aid of the rifle barrel as a lever they had been able to bring a whole wall crashing down, to choke the passage. That had brought silence. For a time, at least, pursuit had been abandoned. In the sliding, dusty avalanche of the wall, hurled down the stairway, Stern knew by the grunts and shrieks which had arisen that some of the Horde had surely perished -- how many, he could not tell. A score or two at the very least, he ardently hoped.

Fear, at any rate, had been temporarily injected into the rest. For the attack had not yet been renewed. Outside in the forest, no sign of the Horde, no sound. A disconcerting, ominous calm had settled like a pall. Even the birds, recovered from their terrors, had begun to hop about and take up their twittering little household tasks.

As in a kind of clairvoyance, the engineer seemed to know there would be respite until night. For a little while, at least, there could be rest and peace. But when darkness should have settled down --

"If they'd only show themselves!" thought he, his leaden eyes closing in an overmastering lassitude, a vast swooning weakness of blood-loss and exhaustion. Not even his parched thirst, a veritable torture now, could keep his thoughts from wandering. "If they'd tackle again, I could score with -- with lead -- what's that I'm thinking? I'm not delirious, am I?"

For a moment he brought himself back with a start, back to a full realization of the place. But again the drowsiness gained on him.

"We've got guns now; guns and ammunition," thought he. "We -- could pick them off -- from the windows. Pick them -- off -- pick -- them -- off -- "

He slept. Thus, often, wounded soldiers sleep, with troubled dreams, on the verge of renewed battle which may mean their death, their long and wakeless slumber.

He slept. And the girl, laying his gashed head gently back upon the pile of furs, bent over him with infinite compassion. For a long minute, hardly breathing, she watched him there. More quickly came her breath. A strange new light shone in her eyes.

"Only for me, those wounds!" she whispered slowly. "Only for me!"

Taking his head in both her hands, she kissed him as he lay unconscious. Kissed him twice, and then a third time.

Then she arose.

Quickly, as though with some definite plan, she chose from among their store of utensils a large copper kettle, one which he had brought her the week before from the little Broadway shop.

She took a long rawhide rope, braided by Stern during their long evenings together. This she knotted firmly to the bale of the kettle.

The revolvers, fully reloaded, she examined with care. One of them she laid beside the sleeper. The other she slid into her full, warm bosom, where the clinging tiger-skin held it ready for her hand.

Then she walked noiselessly to the door leading into the hallway.

Here for a moment she stood, looking back at the wounded man. Tears dimmed her eyes, yet they were very glad.

"For your sake, now, everything!" she said. "Everything -- all! Oh, Allan, if you only knew! And now -- good-by!"

Then she was gone.

And in the silent room, their home, which out of wreck and chaos they had made, the fevered man lay very still, his pulses throbbing in his throat.

Outside, very far, very faint in the forests, a muffled drum began to beat again.

And the slow shadows, lengthening across the floor, told that evening was drawing nigh.

27. To Work!

The engineer awoke with a start -- awoke to find daylight gone, to find that dusk had settled, had shrouded the whole place in gloom.

Confused, he started up. He was about to call out, when prudence muted his voice. For the moment he could not recollect just what had happened or where he was; but a vast impending consciousness of evil and of danger weighed upon him. It warned him to keep still, to make no outcry. A burning thirst quickened his memory.

Then his comprehension returned. Still weak and shaken, yet greatly benefited by his sleep, he took a few steps toward the door. Where was the girl? Was he alone? What could all this mean?

"Beatrice! Oh, Beatrice!" he called thickly, in guarded tones. "Where are you? Answer me!"

"Here -- coming!" he heard her voice. And then he saw her, dimly, in the doorway.

"What is it? Where have you been? How long have I been asleep?"

She did not answer his questions, but came quickly to him, took his hand, and with her own smoothed his brow.

"Better, now?" asked she.

"Lots! I'll be all right in a little while. It's nothing. But what have you been doing all this time?"

"Come, and I'll show you." She led him toward the other room.

He followed, in growing wonder.

"No attack, yet?"

"None. But the drums have been beating for a long time now. Hear that?"

They listened. To them drifted a dull, monotonous sound, harbinger of war.

Stern laughed bitterly, chokingly, by reason of his thirst.

"Much good their orchestra will do them," said he, "when it comes to facing soft-nosed .38's! But tell me, what was it you were going to show me?"

Quickly she went over to their crude table, took up a dish and came back to him.

"Drink this!" bade she.

He took it, wondering.

"What? Coffee? But -- "

"Drink! I've had mine, already. Drink!"

Half-stupefied, he obeyed. He drained the whole dish at a draft, then caught his breath in a long sigh.

"But this means water!" cried he, with renewed vigor. "And -- ?"

"Look here," she directed, pointing. There on the circular hearth stood the copper kettle, three-quarters full.

"Water! You've got water?" He started forward in amazement. "While I've been sleeping? Where -- ?"

She laughed with real enjoyment.

"It's nothing," she disclaimed. "After what you've done for me, this is the merest trifle, Allan. You know that big cavity made by the boiler-explosion? Yes? Well, when we looked down into it, before we ventured out to the spring, I noticed a good deal of water at the bottom, stagnant water, that had run out of the boiler and settled on the hard clay floor and in among the cracked cement. I just merely brought up some, and strained and boiled it, that's all. So you see -- "

"But, my Lord!" burst out the man, "d'you mean to say you -- you went down there -- alone?"

Once more the girl laughed.

"Not alone," she answered. "One of the automatics was kind enough to bear me company. Of course the main stairway was impassable. But I found another way, off through the east end of the building and down some stairs we haven't used at all, yet. They may be useful, by the way, in case of -- well -- a retreat. Once I'd reached the arcade, the rest was easy. I had that leather rope tied to the kettle handle, you see. So all I had to do was -- "

"But the Horde! The Horde?"

"None of them down there, now -- that is, alive. None when I was there. All at the war-council, I imagine. I just happened to strike it right, you see. It wasn't anything. We simply had to have water, so I went and got some, that's all."

"That's all?" echoed Stern, in a trembling voice. "That's -- all!"

Then, lest she see his face even by the dim light through the window, he turned aside a minute. For the tears in his eyes, he felt, were a weakness which he would not care to reveal.

But presently he faced the girl again.

"Beatrice," said he, "words fall so flat, so hopelessly dead; they're so inadequate, so anticlimactic at a time like this, that I'm just going to skip them all. It's no use thanking you, or analyzing this thing, or saying any of the commonplace, stupid things. Let it pass. You've got water, that's enough. You've made good, where I failed. Well -- "

His voice broke again, and he grew silent. But she, peering at him with wonder, laid a hand upon his shoulder.

"Come," said she, "you must eat something, too. I've got a little supper ready. After that, the Pulverite?"

He started as though shot.

"That's so! I can make it now!" cried he, new life and energy suffusing him. "Even with my one hand, if you help me, I can make it! Supper? No, no! To work!"

But she insisted, womanlike; and he at last consented to a bite. When this was over, they began preparations for the manufacture of the terrible explosive, Stern's own secret and invention, which, had not the cataclysm intervened, would have made him ten times over a millionaire. More precious now to him, that knowledge, than all the golden treasures of the dead, forsaken world!

"We've got to risk a light," said he. "If it's turned low, and shaded, maybe they won't learn our whereabouts. But however that may be, we can't work in the dark. It would be too horribly perilous. One false move, one wrong combination, even the addition of one ingredient at the improper moment, and -- well -- you understand."

She nodded.

"Yes," said she. "And we don't want to quit -- just yet!"

So they lighted the smaller of their copper lamps, and set to work in earnest.

On the table, cleared of dishes and of food, Stern placed in order eight glass bottles, containing the eight basic chemicals for his reaction.

Beside him, at his left hand, he set a large metal dish with three quarts of water, still warm. In front of him stood his copper tea-kettle -- the strangest retort, surely in which the terrific compound ever had been distilled.

"Now our chairs, and the lamp," said he, "and we're ready to begin. But first," and, looking earnestly at her, "first, tell me frankly, wouldn't you just a little rather have me carry out this experiment alone? You could wait elsewhere, you know. With these uncertain materials and all the crude conditions we've got to work under, there's no telling what -- might happen.

"I've never yet found a man who would willingly stand by and see me build Pulverite, much less a woman. It's frightful, this stuff is! Don't be ashamed to tell me; are you afraid?"

For a long moment the girl looked at him.

"Afraid -- with you?" said she.

28. The Pulverite

An hour passed. And now, under the circle of light cast by the hooded lamp upon the table, there in that bare, wrecked office-home of theirs, the Pulverite was coming to its birth.

Already at the bottom of the metal dish lay a thin yellow cloud, something that looked like London fog on a December morning. There, covered with the water, it gently swirled and curdled, with strange metallic glints and oily sheens, as Beatrice with a gold spoon stirred it at the engineer's command.

From moment to moment he dropped in a minute quantity of glycerin, out of a glass test-tube, graduated to the hundredth of an ounce. Keenly, under the lamp-shine, he watched the final reaction; his face, very pale and set, reflected a little of the mental stress that bound him.

Along the table-edge before him, limp in its sling, his wounded arm lay useless. Yet with his left hand he controlled the sleeping giant in the dish. And as he dropped the glycerin, he counted.

"Ten, eleven, twelve -- fifteen, sixteen -- twenty! Now! Now pour the water off, quick! Quick!"

Splendidly the girl obeyed. The water ran, foaming strangely, out into a glass jar set to receive it. Her hands trembled not, nor did she hesitate. Only, a line formed between her brows; and her breath, half-held, came quickly through her lips.

"Stop!"

His voice rang like a shot.

"Now, decant it through this funnel, into the vials!"

Again, using both hands for steadiness, she did his bidding.

And one by one as she filled the little flasks of chained death, the engineer stoppered them with his left hand.

When the last was done, Stern drew a tremendous sigh, and

dashed the sweat from his forehead with a gesture of victory.

Into the residue in the dish he poured a little nitric acid.

"That's got no kick left in it, now, anyhow," said he relieved. "The HNO_3 tames it, quick enough. But the bottles -- take care -- don't tip one over, as you love your life!"

He stood up, slowly, and for a moment remained there, his face in the shadow of the lamp-shade, holding to the table-edge for support, with his left hand.

At him the girl looked.

"And now," she began, "now -- ?"

The question had no time for completion. For even as she spoke, a swift little something flicked through the window, behind them.

It struck the opposite wall with a sharp crack! then fell slithering to the floor.

Outside, against the building, they heard another and another little shock; and all at once a second missile darted through the air.

This hit the lamp. Stern grabbed the shade and steadied it. Beatrice stooped and snatched up the thing from where it lay beside the table.

Only one glance Stern gave at it, as she held it up. A long reed stem he saw wrapped at its base with cotton fibers -- a fish-bone point, firm-lashed -- and on that point a dull red stain, a blotch of something dry and shiny.

"Blow-gun darts!" cried he. "Poisoned! They've seen the light -- got our range! They're up there in the tree-tops -- shooting at us!"

With one puff, the light was gone. By the wrist he seized Beatrice. He dragged her toward the front wall, off to one side, out of range.

"The flasks of Pulverite! Suppose a dart should hit one?" exclaimed the girl.

"That's so! Wait here -- I'll get them!"

But she was there beside him as, in the thick dark, he cautiously felt for the deadly things and found them with a hand that dared not tremble. And though here, there, the little venom-stings whis-s-shed over them and past them, to shatter on the rear wall, she helped him bear the vials, all nine of them, to a place of safety in the left-hand front corner where by no possibility could they be struck.

Together then, quietly as wraiths, they stole into the next room; and there, from a window not as yet attacked, they spied out at the dark tree-tops that lay in dense masses almost brushing the walls.

"See? See there?" whispered Stern in the girl's ear. He pointed where, not ten yards away and below, a blacker shadow seemed to move along a hemlock branch. Forgotten now, his wounds. Forgotten his loss of blood, his fever and his weakness. The sight of that creeping stealthy attack nerved him with new vigor. And, even as the girl looked, Stern drew his revolver.

Speaking no further word, he laid the ugly barrel firm across the sill.

Carefully he sighted, as best he could in that gloom lit only by the stars. Coldly as though at a target-shot, he brought the muzzle-sight to bear on that deep, crawling shadow.

Then suddenly a spurt of fire split the night. The crackling report echoed away. And with a bubbling scream, the shadow loosened from the limb, as a ripe fruit loosens.

Vaguely they saw it fall, whirl, strike a branch, slide off, and disappear.

All at once a pattering rain of darts flickered around them. Stern felt one strike his fur jacket and bounce off. Another grazed the girl's head. But to their work they stood, and flinched not.

Now her revolver was speaking, in antiphony with his; and from the branches, two, three, five, eight, ten of the ape-things fell.

"Give it to 'em!" shouted the engineer, as though he had a regiment behind him. "Give it to 'em!" And again he pulled the trigger.

The revolver was empty.

With a cry he threw it down, and, running to where the shot-gun stood, snatched it up. He scooped into his pocket a handful of shells from the box where they were stored; and as he darted back to the window, he cocked both hammers.

145

"Poom! Poom!"

The deep baying of the shotgun roared out in twin jets of flame.

Stern broke the gun and jacked in two more shells.

Again he fired.

"Good Heaven! How many of 'em are there in the trees?" shouted he.

"Try the Pulverite!" cried Beatrice. "Maybe you might hit a branch!"

Stern flung down the gun. To the corner where the vials were standing he ran.

Up he caught one -- he dared not take two lest they should by some accident strike together.

"Here -- here, now, take this!" he bellowed.

And from the window, aiming at a pine that stood seventy-five feet away -- a pine whose branches seemed to hang thick with the Horde's blowgun-men -- he slung it with all the strength of his uninjured arm.

Into the gloom it vanished, the little meteorite of latent death, of potential horror and destruction.

"If it hits 'em, they'll think we are gods, after all, what?" cried the engineer, peering eagerly. But for a moment, nothing happened.

"Missed it!" he groaned. "If I only had my right arm to use now, I might -- "

Far below, down there a hundred feet beneath them and out a long way from the tower base, night yawned wide in a burst of hellish glare.

A vast conical hole of flame was gouged in the dark. For a fraction of a second every tree, limb, twig stood out in vivid detail, as that blue-white glory shot aloft.

All up through the forest the girl and Stern got a momentary glimpse of little, clinging Things, crouching misshapen, hideous.

Then, as a riven and distorted whirl burst upward in a huge geyser of annihilation, came a detonation that ripped, stunned, shattered; that sent both the defenders staggering backward from the window.

Darkness closed again, like a gaping mouth that shuts. And all about the building, through the trees, and down again in a titanic, slashing rain fell the wreckage of things that had been stone, and earth, and root, and tree, and living creatures -- that had been -- that now were but one indistinguishable mass of ruin and of death.

After that, here and there, small dark objects came dropping, thudding, crashing down. You might have thought some cosmic gardener had shaken his orchard, his orchard where the plums and pears were rotten-ripe.

"One!" cried the engineer, in a strange, wild, exultant voice.

29. The Battle on the Stairs

Almost like the echo of his shout, a faint snarling cry rose from the corridor, outside. They heard a clicking, sliding, ominous sound; and, with instant comprehension, knew the truth.

"They've got up, some of them -- somehow!" Stern cried. "They'll be at our throats, here, in a moment! Load! Load! You shoot -- I'll give 'em Pulverite!"

No time, now, for caution. While the girl hastily threw in more cartridges, Stern gathered up all the remaining vials of the explosive.

These, garnered along his wounded arm which clasped them to his body, made a little bristling row of death. His left hand remained free, to fling the little glass bombs.

"Come! Come, meet 'em -- they mustn't trap us, here!"

And together they crept noiselessly into the other room and thence to the corridor-door.

Out they peered.

"Look! Torches!" whispered he.

There at the far end of the hallway, a red glare already flickered on the wall around the turn by the elevator-shaft. Already the confused sounds of the attackers were drawing near.

"They've managed to dig away the barricade, somehow," said Stern. "And now they're out for business -- clubs, poisoned darts and all -- and fangs, and claws! How many of 'em? God knows! A swarm, that's all!"

His mouth felt hot and dry, with fever, and the mad excitement of the impending battle. His skin seemed tense and drawn, especially upon the forehead. As he stood there, waiting, he heard the girl's quick breathing. Though he could hardly see her in the gloom, he felt her presence and he loved it.

"Beatrice," said he, and for a moment his hand sought hers, "Beatrice, little girl o' mine, if this is the big finish, if we both go down together and there's no to-morrow, I want to tell you now -- "

A yapping outcry interrupted him. The girl seized his arm. Brighter the torchlight grew.

"Allan!" she whispered. "Come back, back, away from here. We've got to get up those stairs, there, at the other end of the hall. This is no kind of place to meet them -- we're exposed, here. There's no protection!"

"You're right." he answered. "Come!"

Like ghosts they slid away, noiselessly, through the enshrouding gloom.

Even as they gained the shelter of the winding stairway, the scouts of the Horde, flaring their torches into each room they passed, came into view around the corner at the distant end.

Shuffling, hideous beyond all words by the fire-gleam, bent, wizened, blue, the Things swarmed toward them in a vague and shifting mass, a ruck of horror.

The defenders, peering from behind the broken balustrade, could hear the guttural jabber of their beast-talk, the clicking play of their fangs; could see the craning necks, the talons that held spears, bludgeons, blow-guns, even jagged rocks.

Over all, the smoky gleams wavered in a ghastly interplay of light and darkness. Uncanny shadows leaped along the walls. From every corner and recess and black, empty door, ghoulish shapes seemed creeping.

Tense, now, the moment hung.

Suddenly the engineer bent forward, staring.

"The chief!" he whispered. And as he spoke, Beatrice aimed.

There, shambling among the drove of things, they saw him clearly for a moment: Uglier, more incredibly brutal than ever he looked, now, by that uncanny light.

Stern saw -- and rejoiced in the sight -- that the obeah's jaw hung surely broken, all awry. The quick-blinking, narrow-ridded eyes shuttled here, there, as the creature sought to spy out his enemies. The nostrils dilated, to catch the spoor of man. Man, no longer god, but mortal.

One hand held a crackling pine-knot. The other gripped the heft of a stone ax, one blow of which would dash to pulp the stoutest skull.

This much Stern noted, as in a flash; when at his side the girl's revolver spat.

The report roared heavily in that constricted space. For a moment the obeah stopped short. A look of brute pain, of wonder, then of quintupled rage passed over his face. A twitching grin of passion distorted the huge, wounded gash of the mouth. He screamed. Up came the stone ax.

"Again!" shouted Stern. "Give it to him again!"

She fired on the instant. But already, with a chattering howl, the obeah was running forward. And after him, screaming, snarling, foaming till their lips were all a slaver, the pack swept toward them.

Stern dragged the girl away, back to the landing.

"Up! Up!" he yelled.

Then, turning, he hurled the second bomb.

A blinding glare dazzled him. A shock, as of a suddenly unleashed volcano, all but flung him headlong.

Dazed, choked by the gush of fumes that burst in a billowing cloud out along the hall and up the stairs, he staggered forward. Tightly to his body he clutched the remaining vials. Where was Beatrice? He knew not. Everything boomed and echoed in his stunned ears. Below there, he heard thunderous crashes as wrecked walls and floors went reeling down. And ever, all about him, eddied the strangling smoke.

Then, how long after he knew not, he found himself gasping for air beside a window.

"Beatrice!" he shouted with his first breath. Everything seemed strangely still. No sound of pursuit, no howling now. Dead calm. Not even the drum-beat in the forest, far below.

"Beatrice! Where are you? Beatrice!"

His heart leaped gladly as he heard her answer.

"Oh! Are you safe? Thank God! I -- I was afraid -- I didn't know -- "

To him she ran along the dark passageway.

"No more!" she panted. "No more Pulverite here in the building!" pleaded she. "Or the whole tower will fall -- and bury us! No more!"

Stern laughed. Beatrice was unharmed; he had found her.

"I'll sow it broadcast outside," he answered, in a kind of exaltation, almost a madness from the strain and horror of that night, the weakness of his fever and his loss of blood. "Maybe the others, down there still, may need it. Here goes!"

And, one by one, all seven of the bombs he hurled far out and away, to right, to left, straight ahead, slinging them in vast parabolas from the height.

And as they struck one by one, night blazed like noonday; and even to the Palisades the crashing echoes roared.

The forest, swept as by a giant broom, became a jackstraw tangle of destruction.

Thus it perished.

When the last vial of wrath had been out-poured, when silence had once more dropped its soothing mantle and the great brooding dark had come again, "girdled with gracious watchings of the stars," Stern spoke.

"Gods!" he exclaimed exultantly. "Gods we are now to them -- to such of them as may still live. Gods we are -- gods we shall be forever!

"Whatever happens now, they know us. The Great White Gods of Terror! They'll flee before our very look! Unarmed, if we meet a thousand, we'll be safe. Gods!"

Another silence.

Then suddenly he knew that Beatrice was weeping.

And forgetful of all save that, forgetful of his weakness and his wounds, he comforted her -- as only a man can comfort the woman he loves, the woman who, in turn, loves him.

30. Consummation

After a while, both calmer grown, they looked again from the high window.

"See!" exclaimed the engineer, and pointed.

There, far away to westward, a few straggling lights -- only a very few -- slowly and uncertainly were making their way across the broad black breast of the river.

Even as the man and woman watched, one vanished. Then another winked out, and did not reappear. No more than fifteen seemed to reach the Jersey shore, there to creep vaguely, slowly away and vanish in the dense primeval woods.

"Come," said Stern at last. "We must be going, too. The night's half spent. By morning we must be very far away."

"What? We've got to leave the city?"

"Yes. There's no such thing as staying here now. The tower's quite untenable. Racked and shaken as it is, it's liable to fall at any time. But, even if it should stand, we can't live here any more."

"But -- where now?"

"I don't just know. Somewhere else, that's certain. Everything in this whole vicinity is ruined. The spring's gone. Nothing remains of the forest, nothing but horror and death. Pestilence is bound to sweep this place in the wake of such a -- such an affair.

"The sights all about here aren't such as you should see. Neither should I. We mustn't even think of them. Some way or other we can find a path down out of here, away -- away -- "

"But," she cried anxiously, "but all our treasures? All the tools and dishes, all the food and clothing, and everything? All our precious, hard-won things?"

"Nothing left of them now. Down on the fifth floor, at that end of the building, I'm positive there's nothing but a vast hole blown out of the side of the tower. So there's nothing left to salvage. Nothing at all."

"Can you replace the things?"

"Why not? Wherever we settle down we can get along for a few days on what game I can snare or shoot with the few remaining cartridges. And after that -- "

"Yes?"

"After that, once we get established a little, I can come into the city and go to raiding again. What we've lost is a mere trifle compared to what's left in New York. Why, the latent resources of this vast ruin haven't been even touched yet! We've got our lives. That's the only vital factor. With those everything else is possible. It all looks dark and hard to you now, Beatrice. But in a few days -- wait and see!"

"Allan!"

"What, Beatrice?"

"I trust you in everything. I'm in your hands. Lead me."

"Come, then, for the way is long before us. Come!"

Two hours later, undaunted by the far howling of a wolfpack, as the wan crescent of the moon came up the untroubled sky, they reached the brink of the river, almost due west of where the southern end of Central Park had been.

This course, they felt, would avoid any possible encounter with stragglers of the Horde. Through Madison Forest -- or what remained of it -- they had not gone; but had struck eastward from the building, then northward, and so in a wide detour had avoided all the horrors that they knew lay near the wreck of the tower.

The river, flowing onward to the sea as calmly as though pain and death and ruin and all the dark tragedy of the past night, the past centuries, had never been, filled their tired souls and bodies with a grateful peace. Slowly, gently it lapped the wooded shore, where docks and ships had all gone back to nature; the moonlit ripples spoke of beauty, life, hope, love.

Though they could not drink the brackish waters, yet they laved their faces, arms and hands, and felt refreshed. Then for some time in silence they skirted the flood, ever northward, away from the dead city's heart. And the moon rose even higher, higher still, and great thoughts welled within their hearts. The cool night breeze, freshening in from the vast salt wastes of the sea -- unsailed forever now -- cooled their cheeks and soothed the fever of their thoughts.

Where the grim ruin of Grant's Tomb looked down upon the river, they came at length upon a strange, rude boat, another, then a third -- a whole flotilla, moored with plaited ropes of grass to trees along the shore.

"These must certainly be the canoes of the attacking force from northward, the force that fought the Horde the night before we took a hand in the matter; fought, and were beaten, and -- devoured," said Stern.

And with a practical eye, wise and cool even despite the pain of his wounded arm, he examined three or four of the boats as best he could by moonlight.

The girl and he agreed on one to use.

"Yes, this looks like the most suitable," judged the engineer, indicating a rough, banca-like craft nearly sixteen feet long, which had been carved and scraped and burned out of a single log.

He helped Beatrice in, then cast off the rope. In the bottom lay six paddles of the most degraded state of workmanship. They showed no trace of decoration whatsoever, and the lowest savages of the pre-cataclysmic era had invariably attempted some crude form of art on nearly every implement.

The girl took up one of the paddles.

"Which way? Up-stream?" asked she. "No, no, you mustn't even try to use that arm."

"Why paddle at all?" Stern answered. "See here."

He pointed where a short and crooked mast lay, unstopped, along the side. Lashed to it was a sail of rawhides, clumsily caught together with thongs, heavy and stiff, yet full of promise.

Stern laughed.

"Back to the coracle stage again," said he. "Back to Caesar's time, and way beyond!" And he lifted one end of the mast. "Here we've got the Seuvian *pellis pro velis*, the 'skins for sails' all over again -- only more so. Well, no matter. Up she goes!"

Together they stepped the mast and spread the sail. The engineer took his place in the stern, a paddle in his left hand. He dipped it, and the ripples glinted away.

"Now," said he, in a voice that left no room for argument, "now, you curl up in the tiger-skin and go to sleep! This is my job."

The sail caught the breath of the breeze. The banca moved slowly forward, trailing its wake like widening lines of silver in the moonlight.

And Beatrice, strong in her trust of him, her confidence and love, lay down to sleep while the wounded man steered on and on, and watched her and protected her. And over all the stars, a glory in the summer sky, kept silent vigil.

Dawn broke, all a flame of gold and crimson, as they landed in a sheltered little bay on the west shore.

Here, though the forest stood unbroken in thick ranges all along the background, it had not yet invaded the slope that led back from the pebbly beach. And through the tangle of what once must have been a splendid orchard, they caught a glimpse of white walls overgrown with a mad profusion of wild roses, wisterias and columbines.

"This was once upon a time the summer-place, the big concrete bungalow and all, of Harrison Van Amburg. You know the billionaire, the wheat man? It used to be all his in the long ago. He built it for all time of a material that time can never change. It was his. Well, it's ours now. Our home!"

Together they stood upon the shelving beach, lapped by the river. Somewhere in the woods behind them a robin was caroling with liquid harmony.

Stern drew the rude boat up. Then, breathing deep, he faced the morning.

"You and I, Beatrice," said he, and took her hand. "Just you -- and I!"

"And love!" she whispered.

"And hope, and life! And the earth reborn. The arts and sciences, language and letters, truth, 'all the glories of the world' handed down through us!

"Listen! The race of men, our race, must live again -- shall live! Again the forests and the plains shall be the conquest of our blood. Once more shall cities gleam and tower, ships sail the sea, and the world go on to greater wisdom, better things!

"A kinder and a saner world this time. No misery, no war, no poverty, woe, strife, creeds, oppression, tears -- for we are wiser than those other folk, and there shall be no error."

He paused, his face irradiate. To him recurred the prophecy of Ingersoll, the greatest orator of that other time. And very slowly he spoke again:

"Beatrice, it shall be a world where thrones have crumbled and where kings are dust. The aristocracy of idleness shall reign no more! A world without a slave. Man shall at last be free!

"'A world at peace, adorned by every form of art, with music's myriad voices thrilled, while lips are rich with words of love and truth. A world in which no exile sighs, no prisoner mourns; a world on which the gibbet's shadow shall not fall.

"'A race without disease of flesh or brain, shapely and fair, the wedded harmony of form and function. And as I look, life lengthens, joy deepens, and over all in the great dome shines the eternal star of human hope!'"

"And love?" she smiled again, a deep and sacred meaning in her words. Within her stirred the universal motherhood, the hope of everything, the call of the unborn, the insistent voice of the race that was to be.

"And love!" he answered, his voice now very tender, very grave.

Tired, yet strong, he looked upon her. And as he looked his eyes grew deep and eager.

Sweet as the honey of Hymettus was the perfume of the orchard, all a powder of white and rosy blooms, among which the bees, pollen-dusted, labored, at their joyous, fructifying task. Fresh, the morning breeze. Clear, warm, radiant, the sun of June; the summer sun uprising far beyond the shining hills.

Life everywhere -- and love!

Love, too, for them. For this man, this woman, love; the mystery, the pleasure and the eternal pain.

With his unhurt arm he circled her. He bent, he drew her to him, as she raised her face to his.

And for the first time his mouth sought hers.

Their lips, long hungry for this madness, met there and blended in a kiss of passion and of joy.

ALSO FROM LEONAUR

AVAILABLE IN SOFTCOVER OR HARDCOVER WITH DUST JACKET

SF1 CLASSIC SCIENCE FICTION SERIES
BEFORE ADAM & Other Stories
by Jack London

Volume 1 of The Collected Science Fiction & Fantasy of Jack London.

SOFTCOVER : **ISBN 1-84677-008-4**
HARDCOVER : **ISBN 1-84677-015-7**

SF2 CLASSIC SCIENCE FICTION SERIES
THE IRON HEEL & Other Stories
by Jack London

Volume 2 of The Collected Science Fiction & Fantasy of Jack London.

SOFTCOVER : **ISBN 1-84677-004-1**
HARDCOVER : **ISBN 1-84677-011-4**

SF3 CLASSIC SCIENCE FICTION SERIES
THE STAR ROVER & Other Stories
by Jack London

Volume 3 of The Collected Science Fiction & Fantasy of Jack London.

SOFTCOVER : **ISBN 1-84677-006-8**
HARDCOVER : **ISBN 1-84677-013-0**

WF1 THE WARFARE FICTION SERIES
NAPOLEONIC WAR STORIES
by Sir Arthur Quiller-Couch

Tales of soldiers, spies, battles & Sieges from the Peninsular & Waterloo campaigns

SOFTCOVER : **ISBN 1-84677-003-3**
HARDCOVER : **ISBN 1-84677-014-9**

www.ingramcontent.com/pod-product-compliance
Lightning Source LLC
Chambersburg PA
CBHW030516260626
47157CB00005B/1773